THIS ONE
BECAUSE OF
THE DEAD

THIS ONE
BECAUSE OF
THE DEAD

STORIES BY
LAURE BAUDOT

Cormorant Books

Canada Council   Conseil des Arts
for the Arts   du Canada

 ONTARIO | ONTARIO   Canadian   Patrimoine
CREATES | CRÉATIF   Heritage   canadien

The publisher gratefully acknowledges the support of the Canada Council
for the Arts and the Ontario Arts Council for its publishing program. We
acknowledge the financial support of the Government of Canada through the
Canada Book Fund (CBF) for our publishing activities, and the Government of
Ontario through Ontario Creates, an agency of the Ontario Ministry of Culture,
and the Ontario Book Publishing Tax Credit Program.

LIBRARY AND ARCHIVES CANADA CATALOGUING IN PUBLICATION

Baudot, Laure
[Short stories. Selections]
This one because of the dead / Laure Baudot.

Short stories.
Issued in print and electronic formats.
ISBN 978-1-77086-514-3 (softcover).— ISBN 978-1-77086-515-0 (html)

I. Title.

PS8603.A897A6 2019   C813'.6   C2018-900024-4
                                               C2018-900025-2

Cover photo and design: angeljohnguerra.com
Interior text design: Tannice Goddard, tannicegdesigns.ca
Printer: Friesens

Printed and bound in Canada.

CORMORANT BOOKS INC.
260 SPADINA AVENUE, SUITE 502, TORONTO, ON M5T 2E4
www.cormorantbooks.com

To Leeor — muse, companion, adventurer —
and to our intrepid children:
Rachel, Nathan, and Simon. With love.

CONTENTS

THIS ONE
BECAUSE OF
THE DEAD

THIS ONE BECAUSE OF THE DEAD

ON THE NIGHT BEFORE Akash leaves for Everest, Julie cooks for him a dish his grandmother has taught her. He gobbles the cubed pumpkin and wilted greens. "Delicious, Jules."

Normally this statement would thrill her. She's innovated on Punjabi cooking, jokes that she makes "*Nouveau* Indian." But tonight she's getting that familiar feeling, that stiffness in her jaw. Their conversations accumulate, each one a domino falling against the next, pieces piled up at the base of her skull.

"Don't start," he says.

He's right not to go into it. Acknowledging her anxiety will weaken both of them. Like when she first went up *en pointe* in ballet: she pictured herself falling, and then she did.

Six months ago, against her better judgment, she'd asked if she could come to base camp.

"Terrible idea," he'd said.

As she'd expected.

Increasingly over the past year, she'd been asking the thing she shouldn't. The thing he didn't want her to. The thing she had to admit to herself she knew better than to bring up. She could hear the irritation in his voice when he perceived her as trying to hold him back.

Akash's voice softens. "It's all good, Jules."

He leaves his empty plate on the table and crosses the hall into their home office. The office chair's wheels whirr against the hardwood floor. He's browsing at the computer, looking not only at mountaineering pages with details of Everest's southern route, but also at financial sites with the earnings of the companies he invests in to fund his expeditions.

From this moment on he will be increasingly quiet. She will become most aware of his silence around ten p.m., which is when he will go to bed. Tomorrow morning, just before leaving, he'll joke with her, sounding like his usual self: relaxed, but with an undercurrent of watchfulness.

She is left in the dining room with the scent of old oil, onions, and cumin. Across the hall the computer mouse clicks like a metronome losing time.

HE CAUGHT HER ATTENTION the first time she saw him, five years before. She was filled with anticipation, a sense that here was someone different from the men she sometimes dated. They were working at a satellite call centre and Akash was a team leader, liked by everyone. He wore thin, wool sports shirts that showed off the definition of his upper back. Julie sat in a cubicle behind him and to his left, a position from which she could see the bristles of his crew cut above his tan nape. She learned later that, although he had been brought up Sikh, he was not religious and had cut his hair in his late teens.

A co-worker saw her watching, and said, "He does this crazy-assed mountain stuff."

Julie insinuated herself into his life. She made sure she sat beside him at pub nights, and joined him and his climbing friends for after-gym beers. She told him that she'd always been fascinated by rock climbing, and was elated by their bantering: instead of the vocabulary of single, downtown urbanites — "condo," "storage," "paycheque," — she heard the diction of climbing — "pitch," "belay," "boulder." She didn't understand a word of what they said, but she loved being on the cusp of learning a whole new language. Julie also realized that she had not witnessed people so immersed in their field of expertise since her dancing days.

After he refused to meet her on a Sunday for the third time in a row, she remembered he had told her before they were dating that on Sundays he had dinner with his family. When he finally invited her home for family dinner, she felt as if she had won the lottery. Her parents' idea of togetherness was going out to Morton's steakhouse once a month. In Akash's huge family, in the enormous sit-down dinners where family members bantered and cheered each other on, she saw another example of how a family could be.

One day, after they had been dating for a year, she was felled by a cold. She didn't want him to see her sick, but he came into her apartment as if he assumed she wouldn't refuse him, and seemed to ignore her unbrushed hair and a nose that was red and peeling from too much blowing.

He brought her grocery store chicken soup. She was pleased, but puzzled. "What do you get for yourself when you're sick?"

Akash disappeared into the kitchen. A few minutes later, he returned with a mug of hot, thick milk. A drink he had been given as a child, it was supposed to soothe a sore throat. He took it to her in bed, on a tray, with paper towels he had folded into triangles. It left a pasty, sweet aftertaste on her tongue that was not unpleasant.

For the next two days, he brought her movies and magazines and made sure she was comfortable. She, who had witnessed the competitiveness of the ballet world, now saw evidence that even someone as pre-occupied with himself as Akash could, at times, be quite aware of others. He could be both ambitious and a good person.

AS SOON AS AKASH stops browsing online, he feels the tautness of his limbs. He wants to be on the mountain already. Peaks, unlike loved ones, are easy. Starting a climb is always difficult, but as he gradually gives himself up to it, everything else in his life is eliminated. Sometimes he feels as if he and a mountain are playing a chess game. The mountain is a great but generous opponent — it always lets Akash win.

The days leading up to an expedition are terrible. Exercising would help, but tonight he can't, for fear of overexertion. He goes to the living room, where an enormous rucksack and a small knapsack sit on the carpet. Save for a mattress and jumar, which he'll buy in Kathmandu, he's taking all his equipment. He has created layers: the sharp items (including crampons and an ice pick, its tip covered by a guard) at the bottom of each bag, followed by footwear, bottles, carabiners, ropes, harnesses, helmet, and freeze-dried snacks. Rolled-up clothes in every crevice. No need to unpack to check if he has everything; he used a packing list on his cellphone, created years ago and updated for each expedition. He runs his index finger along each bag, listens to the rustle of the nail as it drags along the nylon.

AKASH WAS NEITHER SOLITARY nor social, but could adapt to circumstances. He felt himself apart from his co-workers because of his hobby. He was always friendly, but had learned long before not to go in depth about climbing; he found most people were either frightened or almost morbidly interested, asking him about accidents on the mountains. As for Julie, her curiosity seemed more genuine than what he was used to encountering; in time he answered her questions about mountaineering with increasingly detailed answers, and she responded eagerly.

The first time Akash really talked to Julie, it was at a pub night organized by their co-workers. In order to accommodate his then-training schedule, he arrived early so he could leave early enough to get to bed on time. He sat at one of the wood-panelled booths and thought he was there before everyone else, until Julie shimmied in beside him.

He had noticed Julie before because she seemed to hold herself apart, didn't join in the office gossip. Her long hair reminded him of the heavy gold necklaces his grandmother wore. When she leaned over to study the menu, her hair wafted patchouli, familiar and comforting. It was only later that he wondered if she had come early in order to look for him.

In the course of conversation, he told her he went home every weekend, for dinner with his parents and grandmother. At first, she seemed not to believe him. Then, she was astonished. "That's so nice."

He asked her where her parents lived and she waved vaguely in the direction of downtown. "They have their own lives."

He swigged his beer. "To tell the truth, I wish mine wouldn't expect so much."

Akash found that he enjoyed being with her; she was a change of pace. After three months, he took her home for Sunday dinner and introduced her to his family. They, having been afraid that he would never find a girlfriend, took Julie in like a daughter. They would have preferred a wife, but counted their blessings.

One Sunday, he came to his parents' home to find Julie already in the kitchen, cooking with his grandmother. Her hair was in a ponytail, a wisp sticking out from her forehead. She looked happy.

"Your grandmother is teaching me curries from scratch."

His grandmother, a tiny woman with a gold nose ring, said, "We are learning."

The kitchen steamed, the pots bubbled with ghee and spices. In her bare feet and apron, Julie seemed to fit right in. The discomfort in Akash's gut was replaced with a feeling of pleasure, and when his grandmother and his girlfriend turned back to the stove, he thought, *My women.*

A FEW WEEKS INTO Julie and Akash's relationship, Akash's climbing partner Singleton, who lived in Calgary, came to visit. He was of Irish stock, with fish-belly-white skin, marble-blue eyes, and a lined forehead, and he talked to Akash as though Julie were not there. "You've got to come out, man. I could set you up with the business. You could make a little money, take time off to climb."

The swiftness of Julie's rage surprised her. Until then she had felt as if she alone understood Akash, but she saw that she had been mistaken, that there was a whole other relationship in his life. Her throat closed.

Akash nodded. "Work offered me a position. Opportunity to open a new office."

"You should get with that."

Julie stared. "When was this?"

Akash's head swivelled toward her. "I'm not going."

"Do it!" said Singleton.

Akash took a few gulps of beer. "My mother would kill me."

Singleton peered at Julie for what seemed to be the first time. "You factor into this too, don't you?" He seemed both resigned and bemused. Akash smiled and reddened, and Julie's jaw relaxed.

It was only when he took her climbing at a local gym that she began to doubt she could fully enter his world. She could never make it to the top of a climb. At the base of each route, she would visualize her success and start climbing, and each time, when she reached the halfway point, her body would thwart her progress. Her legs trembled and her heart sped up. The only thing that could unlock her muscles and allow her to make the reverse journey was Akash's voice, talking her down.

Once she was on the ground, he would turn his attention to his own ascent. He neither complained about her lack of progress nor encouraged her to improve, exhibiting a degree of ambivalence that worried her.

SINGLETON WAS THE UNCLE of Akash's undergraduate roommate. When he and Akash first met, Akash bragged about his prowess in investing his family's education savings. Mostly mid-risk stuff, but when he tried high-risk ventures, he found that his stocks rose more often than they fell.

"It's insane," he said to his new friend. They were in a pub, waiting for Singleton's nephew. "Everything I do works."

"The gods are smiling on you?" Singleton said, and drank some beer. "You do some climbing. You'll find your edge."

So Akash went out west, and they climbed Mount Athabasca together. For the first two days, Singleton — a mountaineering guide — gave him lessons. By day three it was clear that

Akash was a natural, hauling himself up the mountain face as though he were putting together a puzzle. Akash experienced the same sensation climbing that he did when he traded stocks: despite the possibility of losing everything, he was certain it wouldn't happen to him, because he was that good, because of the God-given talents he spoke of when he'd first met Singleton.

Over time, however, he came to understand that the edge Singleton had been referring to was not Akash's aptitude — at least not solely; he was referring to luck, and the fact that Akash needed to believe in it if he was going to climb mountains.

Over the years, they discussed the seven summits, including Everest, which all serious mountaineers wanted to ascend. Akash didn't see the point of Everest. Too famous, too crowded. Singleton disagreed. In 1963, when he was nine years old, he'd witnessed the highly publicized news that Hornbein and Unsoeld had made the first ascent of Everest's West Ridge. Everest hadn't yet happened for Singleton. Now he wanted to climb it with Akash.

"Highest peak is highest peak. And the beauty? Seriously. There's plenty of time for new routes. You're a young buck."

He finally persuaded Akash by telling him that it would make him marketable. "The sponsors, man. Think of this as an investment into your future climbs."

IN THE END, HOWEVER, Singleton is not accompanying Akash. Three years before, when they climbed Mount Elbrus,

Singleton suffered serious altitude sickness and couldn't recover in time to train for Everest. By then Akash had already spent months soliciting sponsors and training; he couldn't afford to give up. For the first time in eight years, he will climb without his partner.

JULIE TRIED SEVERAL TIMES to dissuade Akash from Everest.

"Not this one," she said.

This one because of the dead. Those bodies that, along with human excrement and empty oxygen canisters, litter the mountain. She thinks of Mount Elbrus, and how Akash had come home with his extremities frost-nipped. They had joked about it. She had told him how, when she was in ballet school, the girls' toenails blackened and fell off. He teased her about how she pronounced it "baaaa-lay," lengthening and emphasizing the first syllable, which seemed to him to convey the upper-class-ness of that world.

Until she saw an Everest documentary, she had no idea of the extent of the carnage. One corpse was named "Green Boots" because his footwear stuck out of the ice like fluorescent hard candy. Another body, an almost-bald skull denuded by time, seemed to have acquired the colour and texture of a naked Barbie. The camera focused on this body as strands of hair lifted and fell in the wind.

Over several weeks, Julie tried to change Akash's mind. Even as she saw that he was becoming annoyed, she kept insisting. She couldn't help herself.

IN BED, AKASH TURNS away from Julie. He knows his cold-
ness hurts her, but he can't give her anything of himself. To
speak means breaking his fragile self-containment. He holds
his body and mind apart, hoarding their energy for the task
ahead. He works to keep frightening images at bay. Each night
before a trip, he's haunted by mishaps that could be had
on a mountain. The memory of Singleton, corpse-like, carried
on a stretcher down Mount Elbrus. He blocks out the negative
imagery by picturing the route he's plotted to take up Everest.
In his mind he realizes each step, all the way to the peak.

THE NEXT MORNING AKASH appears calm in Julie's eyes.
He's speaking to her again.

"Be good, eh?"

"Pfft." She makes a dismissive motion with her hand. By
now she's used to the whole routine, and it's never good to
part on a bad note.

Akash smiles. "I'm hoping something happens to the Creature while I'm away."

The Creature is Akash's name for Julie's cat, Nureyev,
who is very sick and who, Akash has argued, needs to be
put out of its misery.

When the cab pulls up in front of their house, Akash
kisses her on the temple and pulls her to him briefly. He
bounces as he walks to the car. Julie goes back into the house
and sits down on the living room knotted rug. She listens to
the car's thrum turn into a roar, and then fade.

WHEN JULIE WAS TEN, she watched Larissa Lezhnina as Princess Aurora dance in a video production of *Sleeping Beauty*, watched during the *grand pas de deux* as Lezhnina spun *en pointe*, her supporting leg strong, her extended leg so long it seemed to float off the stage. She didn't recognize what Lezhnina had inspired in that moment until much later, when she read a reproduction of Karen Kain's childhood journal in which the eight-year-old had written, *I'm going to be a famous ballerina*. It was the naïve certainty of a child for whom a goal and a desire for the goal weren't yet separate concepts.

She auditioned for the National Ballet School, but didn't get in. She attended the lesser known, but still rigorous, George Brown School of Dance. Every day after school, her nanny would take her there on the streetcar from King Street subway station.

When she turned eleven, she started going to ballet alone. She stopped off at McDonald's to eat a carton of fries before class. Skinny and careless, she downed the fries every weekday for a year, not associating her chronic constipation with the four pounds of potatoes consumed weekly. When the other girls started pointing out the layer of fat that had developed on her hips, she forced herself to stop eating the fries, replacing them with a daily consumption of muffins from a corner store. Then she heard the girls gossip in the change room about her new choice of food, and she started throwing out the muffins after eating a few bites.

Now Julie teaches dance at a private girls' art school, where she sought refuge after what she considers to be her wasted years at the call centre. Here the girls sidle up to her in the hope that she can help them achieve careers in dance. They always seem to crop up during Julie's lunch hour.

This time, a girl named Melissa stands at her office door. Julie puts her fork down. The smell of fish and chips and vinegar — which she now consumes, carefully, once a week — fills the tiny, airless room.

"I was wondering," says Melissa, "if I could get into George Brown?"

Normally Melissa is plain-looking, with small, almond-shaped eyes and pale parchment skin. But when she's dancing, Julie can't take her eyes off the girl. Melissa is miles beyond her classmates. Julie watches her and forgets that effort is involved, that she has mass — muscles, bones, tendons.

Julie remembers a girl who went to her ballet school. The teacher would always point her out. "Watch," she would say. "The extension, the feet." And the other girls, who moments before had felt airborne, would then experience the heaviness of their limbs, the work involved in the dance.

Julie runs through some calculations. Three more years at four hours per weeknight, plus six hours of class on Saturday. With the help of some open-minded teachers, Melissa has a chance of becoming a company apprentice.

"My parents think it's too much pressure." Melissa says this coyly, as if she expects Julie to contradict her.

Julie remembers the rounds and rounds of food talk that took place in her old change room. Waists were measured with tailors' tape, half centimetre by half centimetre. The girls were watchful for the dangers of carbs. The fries Julie eats today are saturated with that tang of guilt. On the night her beloved-and-feared principal asked her to leave the school forever, Julie stopped at McDonald's and bought an extra-large fries. Bending the fries until they splintered, she saw her own self break. But the fries were delicious, despite being broken: the salty crunch of the crust; the starchy, steaming mash; the aftertaste of oil lingering on her tongue.

"Your parents are right," Julie says, and hands Melissa a tissue.

The kick her student executes against the doorjamb causes only a muted thud because of the fireproofing. "You don't know what it's like to want something so bad," she says as she leaves.

"I do," Julie says out loud, her words empty in the vinegary air of her office.

AT BASE CAMP, FACED with the sun, cobalt sky, and the laundry line of prayer flags flickering in the wind, Akash feels possessed by the place. The hard snow crunches under his boots. Wafts of dry powder from the grey rock and needles of cold air hit his nostrils. His stomach cramps as the altitude shunts the blood away from vital organs; for him, this means nausea and loose bowels. He appreciates this first, familiar assault on his body, for it makes him more self-aware, present in the moment and in his skin.

Akash is staring up at the mountain when Wilson, the guide, walks up to him. He's an American with fifteen years' experience. Two years ago, he summited both Everest and Lhotse in a twenty-four-hour period. Wilson started climbing as a teenager; since Akash didn't start until his late twenties, he figures he has another ten years to go before he measures himself against Wilson.

In front of them is the Khumbu Icefall, seagull-white slabs of icing on a cake.

Wilson follows his glance. "Haven't lost anyone yet."

"Wasn't even entertaining the thought."

Wilson looks back at the camp. "Why Mr. Weekend Warrior chose to make Everest his first, I don't know. Plenty of good basic peaks where he's from." Weekend Warrior is the name they've given to a middle-aged businessman from Utah.

"But it had to be Everest."

"It had to be Everest."

They smile at each other.

"With my help. And that of the gods." Wilson points to the sky.

Akash longs for Singleton's companionship. They have a joint climbing history, with triumphs and disappointments familiar only to them.

AFTER SINGLETON RECOVERED SUFFICIENTLY from Elbrus to be able to talk, Akash apologized for proceeding without him.

Singleton was pragmatic. "It had to happen eventually."

Secretly, Akash had worried; if Singleton's luck had failed once, it could fail again. Or was it Singleton, the man himself, who had failed? If something were to happen to him, he — unlike Singleton — would have recourse. He had family. He had his parents, his mother. He had Julie, his eternal blonde who, after an initial few stuttering advances, would embrace him when he returned.

JULIE'S DAD WAS A corporate lawyer, her mother a charity volunteer. Hers was a solitary childhood; the cat was her main companion. She used to sit in front of the television after ballet, her legs in forward splits with Nureyev in front of her, burying her nose in his fur and woodsy scent.

At the animal hospital, Julie watches the vet listen to Nureyev's heart. The vet has silver hair and high-riding, compassionate eyebrows. The stethoscope bangs onto his chest. "I always leave it to the mom and dad."

Julie tells him that she'll give it a day or two to see how things go.

He shows her how to push an intravenous needle under Nureyev's skin, in the spot between his shoulder blades. "Are you squeamish?"

The dancers' toenails used to fall off, revealing pinkish-green stamps underneath.

"One thing I'm not," Julie says to the vet. She pays the bill and leaves his office.

But she can only hold on to the cat for one more day. Nureyev's fur has started to fall out, he can no longer walk. She cries, blows her nose, picks up the phone. "In the end, I can't watch him suffer anymore," she explains.

In the office, the nurse holds Nureyev and Julie strokes his head. The vet brings a sliver of a needle toward the cat's right foreleg.

Julie stops breathing at the exact moment Nureyev goes still. She is shocked by how little time there is between the injection and his death. The vet leaves her alone with him, and she runs her index finger along his side and his bony back. For what must be a long time, she stands next to Nureyev on the clinic table, eventually sensing his body stiffen. The fur under her fingers suddenly belongs to a taxidermist's model: his torso a cage of something long-ago stuffed.

How quickly a decision is made, thinks Julie. *How rapidly things are lost.*

UNLIKE WILSON, AKASH DOES not carry a satellite phone; it would interfere with his immersion in the expedition. Base camp is his last chance to talk to Julie until after the assault.

Calling her creates a sense of intrusion; she is imposing herself into his aspirations. She has no idea what he's feeling right now. The way his colon is wrecked. His gathering sense of focus. His vision of himself standing on the mountain's peak. She can't understand his addiction to success. At this point, nothing can persuade him to give up this expedition.

She leaps from one worry to another and back. "Do you know anyone there?"

He too repeats himself. "Everyone's alone. Look at Herzog. Simpson. Everyone."

It feels as if another Akash is speaking. He recognizes this other man, who tries to justify his longing to be alone. At the same time, he trembles with the desire to hold Julie, to smell her neck.

"I'll be okay," he says, his voice echoing, doubling itself through Nepal's telecommunications.

WHEN AKASH CALLS HER from base camp, it takes Julie a minute or two to connect his voice to the person she knows, and for her to resume the intimacy of their relationship. It is always like this when they haven't seen each other for a period of time.

She won't tell him about Nureyev. It's too fresh, and she can't bear what will surely be his quick acceptance of her cat's death.

"How's the guide? Do you know anyone there? I kind of wish Singleton were with you." She doesn't like Singleton, but in her absence, Singleton's presence would be comforting. As if he could prevent Akash from hurting himself, or doing something stupid.

The phone line stutters and his sentences are spliced. "One...Herzog...One."

She guesses what he's saying, about everyone being alone. "I've always hated that."

THAT WEEK, IN DANCE class, Melissa barely makes an effort. Her movements seem to parody themselves. Only once is she gripped by the dance and forgets that she is supposed to be angry with Julie. When Julie asks the accompanist to stop playing, Melissa looks bewildered, then glares at her teacher.

For God's sake, thinks Julie. *Let's put things into perspective. Your partner is not on a mountain. Your pet is not dead. Your loves are not disappearing.* "Girls, if you can't concentrate, think hard about why you're here." She is astonished to hear an echo of the old George Brown principal's voice in her own.

Julie remembers the day she was called into the principal's office and was told she could not stay in the program. The principal, Angelina, seemed relieved, as if she had just struck Julie off a list of her competitors.

AKASH'S TEAM IS HAVING dinner in the mess tent. At the end of one of the long foldout tables, the Utah businessman talks with another climber. *The WW*, as Akash has come to think of him, is a large guy with sand-brown hair. He wears an army-green vest with eight pockets, from which he has, at various times, pulled out two kinds of Swiss army knives, a lighter, a ballpoint pen, and a small notebook, on which he takes careful notes. "For my kids," he says. "Hopefully not for posterity, right?" His laugh booms. Then he addresses the group at the table, telling them about his training. "I ran every day with twelve kilograms on my back. Cross-trainer, rowing, biking. Then my trainer would say, 'It's time to start!' All that other stuff, it was only the warm-up!" He leans toward them. "My wife got fed up."

The WW, Akash thinks, *probably got his vest at Tilleys*. Yet he feels some respect for him growing. Their training is almost identical. And, like the American man's wife, Julie had pressured Akash about the time he was committing to the climb. By January, when he was running through the snow, she had started asking him whether he really needed to run "every single day."

Wilson approaches the table. "Ready for day one?"

"About time," says the Utah businessman.

"Take it easy. We'll get you up there but you have to listen to me." He looks around. "Goes for all of you."

He looks nervous; his business depends on ensuring everyone's safety. But people know what they're getting into. Everybody talks. Everybody reads the biographies of old mountaineers, the blogs of climbers whose teammates didn't make it.

Akash would rather give up mountaineering than become a guide. It's hard enough to get yourself up and down in one piece without worrying about someone else. The day of Akash's first summit, on Athabasca's peak, he and Singleton had stood under a layer of cloud puffs. The afternoon's light illuminated Singleton's face, its recently reddened skin, and its grey-stubbled chin. At the thought his mentor was getting old, Akash felt sorry. He also thought about being on his own, of being alone in conquering other peaks, and felt a faint throb of triumph.

ONE OF AKASH'S TEAMMATES is a petite Indo-Canadian woman with a dark-brown, pixie haircut. Like Akash, she is in her late twenties; they are the youngest team members.

A necklace, a gold reproduction of Mount Everest, rests on her breastbone.

Back in Kathmandu, she introduced herself as Ronda. "Raveena, actually. I bullied my parents into calling me Ronda."

"'Beauty of the Sun'?"

She stared. "Did you go to Gurdwara on Sundays?"

"Plus Punjabi school."

They were in a Middle Eastern restaurant, Ronda shovelling down lentil soup faster than he did. Between mouthfuls she told him about her climbing history, how she hustled Indian businesses in order to pay for the expedition.

"Not too many Indian ladies climbing mountains," she said. "That made me highly marketable."

"Nicely done," he said. "Tell me again about Himachal Pradesh." It's a Northern Indian route she mentioned she once took, trekking from Spiti to the Ladakh valleys.

"I felt like I was the only person on Earth."

"Awesome."

"You're wondering how I do it, with children?" she asked. "An organized nanny."

He'd been asking himself who gave her the necklace.

JULIE FILLS HER EVENINGS with appointments — dental, hairdressing, OBGYN. She goes out with colleagues from the school, invited to nip out for ice cream. Hearing the teachers speak of mortgages and complain about the disparity between the numbers of holidays in the private system versus the public sector, she feels like she's going to die of boredom and remembers why she rarely spends time with her co-workers.

Melissa's father calls her at home. Julie is used to students' parents calling her; she works at a private school, and parent-teacher communication is expected. When she looks at her phone's call display and recognizes Melissa's family name, she is wary.

Melissa is bored, Mr. Mackay tells her. He wonders if Julie can find something more stimulating for her, something geared to her zeal for dancing? Something that will dissuade her from wanting to leave this school, with its strong academic strain, for a ballet school? "Although," he adds, wistfully, "I'm beginning to think it's a losing battle."

Julie is touched by Mr. Mackay's attention. He is a good man, invested in his daughter. She begins to feel bad about her refusal to let Melissa grow. She will do her best, she tells him.

DURING ACCLIMATIZING FORAYS UP Everest, Akash is bowled over by Ronda. Climbing up and through the Khumbu Icefall, she finds footholds without hesitation, and takes only a second before she hauls her body up. When she reaches the ladders that are stretched over crevasses, she places her crampons squarely on each rung. Her instinct and flexibility are of a piece. He recognizes in her his own talent, an ability to see both an entire structure, as if from above, as well as its smallest topography. The skill to map a path through a maze, and the physique to carry out that vision.

He prefers inborn talent to hard work, likes witnessing the casual way in which accomplished people wear their skill. It reminds him of when, early in his relationship with Julie, they watched an old video tape of her dancing in a school show. Julie was on a small stage, lit up by a spotlight. She appeared more muscular than the other dancers. As she leapt, her legs seemed to lift her body up by dint of sheer effort. In her bare thighs, which were the size of rugby balls, Akash saw years of training. "Look at you," he'd said, and she laughed, called it a souvenir of youth.

Ronda climbs fast. "I need to be speedy. In and out. No stamina."

It's as though everything in her life slides away, crusts of snow rolling down an icy slope. She understands, as he does, that when she focuses on her goals, things go by the wayside.

JULIE IS WATCHING MELISSA dance. She has given her music to dance solo, a piece she had choreographed herself. Over a few evenings in the school's empty studio, Julie hustled her flabby muscles into movement and created a difficult piece for her student. It was not as hard for her as one would think; the body remembers, after all.

Piqué, tour jetée, chassé, tour jetée. Melissa flies across the floor. When the music stops, Julie has to clear her throat before she can speak. She turns to the girls who are lounging against the studio wall, staring.

"That, ladies, is called dancing."

BACK HOME, AKASH DISCOURAGED Julie from browsing for images of the bodies on Everest. "It's morbid, what you're doing."

Here, he can't avoid them. There are so many. Mummified remains. A bit of skull, a patch of hair. The Gore-Tex horrifies him. Bright pink and stop-sign red jackets found in high-end sports stores, coats worn by housewives and alpinists alike. They speak to him of lost promises, of wealth or adventure. Here they are shrouds. He himself wears a yellow down jacket, which he will never look at in the same way again.

After passing seven corpses, Akash stops counting. From then on, he registers bodies with only a flicker of shock.

On the night of May fifth, they climb with intent to summit. The gap between he and Ronda grows. He likes that she's faster than him. He's not jealous in the way he would be, were she a man. There are words he wants to give her, words that have been flying around in his mind for weeks. Talk of love and admiration and a promise of a life lived together. He will say, "I know it's crazy." He will say, "We are a match."

He hears echoes of his grandmother's talk of marriage being a joining of two souls. Although he's not religious, this idea comforts him. He had always felt cosseted, sheltered by the two principal women in his life, his mother and grandmother — now he feels in himself something that is in step with them.

After ten hours, Akash reaches the Hillary Step, the sheer rock face just before the summit. There is a ladder to climb the Step, and people on each side wait their turn. There are lineups in each direction. He recognizes Ronda by her lime-green jacket. She's coming toward him, stepping off the bottom step of the ladder. Behind her oxygen mask, her eyes seem angry.

"Nice solitude, eh?" Akash pulls down his mask and whispers, chopping up the words with laboured breath.

A smile slits her eyes.

Akash can only imagine feeling elated. Fatigue, oxygen deprivation, and the presence of so many climbers bar the way. He stores this feeling up for later, for when they reach the base — for when they'll be able to talk for real.

ONE LATE EVENING, JULIE takes the subway and a streetcar to the George Brown School of Dance. She has come deliberately late so that the classes will be over. Nevertheless, she catches a glimpse of girls filing out of one of the studios, and smells a combination of rosin, sweat, and clementines, scents so familiar that tears prickle the inside of the bridge of her nose.

On the way to the administrative offices, she hesitates. Instead of taking a right turn, she takes a left, down a hallway, toward the old studios, the ones used by students of the non-professional program. The girls used to call these the "garbage studios" because of the nearby recycling bins, with their stench of soured chocolate milk and orange juice.

She's surprised to see one of the studios is equipped with perfectly respectable bars and mirrors, as well as a grand piano. It has a well-worn wooden floor, the kind no longer found in newer studios. She takes a few tentative dance steps. *Plié, degagée, piqué.* She tries a *fouetté à demi-pointe.* Even though she's wearing blue jeans, her body remembers the motion. Her leg scissors out and in, thrusts her around and around. Her tears are flung out, dried by the speed of her spinning. The image of her long, blonde ponytail flies across all three mirrors.

When she finally stops, it is to hear, above her galloping heart, a familiar voice coming from the doorway of the studio.

"The mistress of *fouettés,*" says Angelina, a huge smile cracking her narrow face open as she stares at Julie.

AKASH WAITS IN LINE for his turn on Everest's thirty-square-foot apex. Once the climber before him heads back toward the south ridge, Akash takes his place. He moves his oxygen mask aside so he can feel the wind on his face. He strives to experience the moment by exposing as much of himself as possible to the elements. In front of him the blue sky is darker than he expected; there are cotton ball clouds and grey-blue peaks patched with snow. At his feet, brimming over the peak, are lines of flags. Below him is a queue of waiting men and women.

He snaps some photos of himself and the view. He's aware he should be elated, but doesn't feel it. *How are all these people here?* he asks himself. *This peak belongs to me.*

JULIE SITS IN ANGELINA's office, a china teacup on the heavy oak desk in front of her.

"I want to hear everything," Angelina says. She looks the same, but older: her bun, now dyed reddish-brown, rides high on her head, and her huge eyes are lined with kohl that looks ghoul-like. Crows' feet spread out from the sides of her eyes.

They talk for an hour. Angelina is still the principal of the dance school. "Until they kick me out," she says. Julie recognizes that old stubbornness, though it doesn't seem as frightening as it used to be. Less like a stone wall and more like the Dutch boy putting his finger in the dike.

"I felt so bad about letting you go," says Angelina. "You tried so hard. I just thought, why go through all that if it's not the right thing for you?"

An old hurt, but it doesn't devastate her in the way she expected. There is a kind of lightening. Space opens up, a parachute billowing from air underneath. Angelina was trying to save her, then, by expelling her. It is possible that what Julie mistook then for spitefulness was actually relief on her behalf.

"But you're happy," Angelina says.

Julie remembers watching Melissa dance the piece she had created and finds that she is, if not happy, then not unhappy. "Actually," Julie leans forward. "I'm here to talk to you about a student."

ON HIS WAY DOWN, Akash reaches the Hillary Step again. He rubs his nose with the back of his hand, looking down to make sure both nose and hand are still there; he hasn't been able to feel them in the last hour. A crust of blood from a nosebleed crumbles on his glove. He is colder than he has ever been in his life. Clipping into a fixed rope, he descends over the lip of the spur.

A few metres below him, on the near-vertical slant, is a red object. The slumped figure of the Utah businessman, held in place by his clip attached to the fixed line.

You gotta be kidding me, Akash thinks.

On the ice below, climbers proceed down the mountain. Above him, a line of waiting men and women forms. He feels the line as something substantial, a giant hand pushing him forward. He flicks his eyes toward the Utah businessman, looking for humidity inside his mask — a telltale sign of breath — and finds none.

Keeping the figure in his periphery, he unclips himself. The man's coat scrapes his own as he climbs over. Akash wants to close his eyes, but can't for fear of falling. A chasm lies on either side of them. The winds buffet his body, and he clips himself in again on the other side of the figure. He wants to get down as fast as possible, but is thwarted by the climbers below him. Akash starts to hyperventilate and, staring straight out at the white vista, tries to quiet his breathing so he doesn't panic. Once he puts some distance between himself and other climbers, he accelerates his descent slightly: only his training prevents him from running all the way down to the next camp.

JULIE GOT AKASH TO agree to call her, forty-eight to seventy-two hours after he reaches the peak. On the day he is supposed to return to base camp, she stays home. She doesn't know how she'll react when she hears his voice. She could burst into tears, or she could feel a vice of rage — at times like this, she doesn't want to be exposed to the world. She doesn't dare leave the house.

She scours the Internet for news and learns from Wilson's team's blog that his team has successfully summited and is on its way down the mountain. The ordeal is not over, she knows; many climbers die on their descent. For the next few hours she returns to the Internet, but there are no more updates.

Akash doesn't call.

Twenty-four hours later, Julie calls in sick to work. She scours the Internet, refreshing and refreshing Wilson's site. That night she sleeps on the couch, her laptop on the floor, within arm's reach. On day three, a few lines appear on Wilson's blog stating that the team is back at base camp. She busies herself in the house, takes a shower and applies makeup, as if by preparing herself she will behave on the call the way a girlfriend should — as someone who shores Akash against calamities. When he still hasn't called by mid-afternoon, she pulls a frozen puri out of her freezer and puts it in the microwave, watches it turn in lazy circles.

She is still at the table, her half-eaten puri on a small plate, when Akash's mother calls. Her strong Punjabi accent gives Julie a rush of familiarity. "Isn't it fabulous?" she says. She chatters about the climb, and Julie slowly comes to understand that she has heard specific details from Akash, that she has been contacted by him, that she has spoken to him.

Julie is so confused by this knowledge that she doesn't respond save for a few "Uh huhs." It's possible that his mother senses this because she asks, sympathetically, how Julie is holding up. As women they need to be okay with their men going off, she says, which strikes Julie as old-fashioned, though typical of his mother. "He has always done what he wants."

After they hang up, Julie continues to sit in the kitchen. The puri dries and curls at its edges. She has realized two things in the last few minutes: one, that when Akash speaks of staying in town for his family, he is really speaking of his love for his mother. Two, that one day, when he leaves, he will not return to Julie.

AKASH AND RONDA ARE back in Kathmandu, in the same Middle Eastern restaurant, sharing a meal and drinking Tuborg. Ronda, whose stomach has not recovered from the altitude, wants soup, soup, and only soup. Akash, who has frost nip on his nose and toes, drinks to dull the pain.

There are images he can't shake. He sees himself unbuckling his harness from the ladder. His stiff hand undoing the clip. There is the figure of a man he can't see clearly. He wants to give these images to someone else, to relieve himself of them, but he's afraid to open his mouth.

There is a commotion in a corner of the room. Someone has entered the restaurant, and people are rising to pat him on the back.

"Who is that?" Akash asks.

Ronda looks over. "Didn't you hear about the Weekend Warrior? He ran out of bottled oxygen and collapsed. That man," she gestures with her chin, "saved his life. Gave up on the summit to unhook him from the Hillary Step and carry him down. He must be crazy strong." They watch as a group invites the man to sit with him. "You gotta hand it to him. Everyone else passed without doing bugger-all."

Akash puts down his bottle, relieved for an opening, but not sure where to start. "I couldn't see a breath."

Ronda stares at him.

He says, "All those bodies. I needed to get out of there." He's whispering now.

For a moment he thinks she sees his point, until she pushes her bowl away.

"Where are you going?" he asks.

"Home," she says, her eyes avoiding his, looking everywhere but at him.

WHEN AKASH FINALLY CALLS, Julie — who is trying not to believe that his silence means he is thinking of leaving her — is astonished. The call is from a regular phone. He is back in Kathmandu, and the reception is clearer than it has been for weeks.

She tries to decide whether she wants to bring up his mother. Julie wonders what will happen if she accuses him of putting his mother before her in the hierarchy of his relationships and, as she does so, she starts a few sentences without completing them.

Akash doesn't notice. He's preoccupied, speaks vaguely of the weather and his fatigue. After a minute, he launches into a mangled explanation of something that happened on the mountain. He mentions extreme chill, danger, and the need for quick decisions. He speaks of responsibility to oneself. He uses the second person pronoun, which confuses her more than she already is.

She tells him to start again with his explanation. "You stepped over a person?"

He asks her to understand why he did what he did. He is a wild animal surrounded by humans, one torn between looking for a way out, and staying because it finds that, after all, it wishes to be tamed.

The beseeching in his voice is new to her. She is filled with desire — not sexual, but a yearning to pull him in and comfort him. Her body, which a few minutes ago was slack, tautens. She feels powerful, magnanimous. At the same time, she wonders how long the note of pleading in Akash's voice will last, and if it will dissipate before he returns to her. She half-guesses that his appeal for help now may shame him into leaving her in the future. She tightens her grip on the phone, as if to postpone the moment when she must surrender her control over him.

"Just come home," she says.

SIBLINGS

THE BLACK-GREEN WATER lapping at the rocks lets no light in. Two girls and a boy stare down at it.

"I'd rather not know," says Sonya.

"What?" Charles asks.

"What's below," she says.

Charles squints at the lake through his bangs, long despite his father's best efforts. "This year we'll do it. We'll swim around the island."

The rough rock warms Sonya's bare feet. The sun is a hand on her nape.

"You think so?" asks Vee, Charles' younger sister. She's looking at Sonya.

The island swim is a rite of passage for kids whose families cottage there. "I'll get you there," Charles tells Sonya.

Charles made grade nine swim team last year, and Vee aims to do the same in two years. Sonya, on the other hand, hates swimming lessons and only just passed an orange badge level several years ago. While brother and sister dove for pucks in the deep end of the pool, Sonya splashed around in shallower water.

But swimming with Charles and Vee will help Sonya fit right into the Remington family. And this year, there is Charles to think of. When she makes it around the island, he will smile at her. *Well done*, he will say, his jaw set in a way that echoes his father's. She will feel the whole of herself, her fears and her sadness, contained in the square of that chin.

Across the bay is Kingston, where they all come from, and where they have left Sonya's mother, Joy, behind in her studio.

"I'll join you guys one of these days," says Joy. "Once I've finished this run."

Joy is a painter, and by "run" she means paintings. Her mother's been working on the same group of paintings for years, as far as she can tell. Sonya isn't sure if she wants her mother to come to the island. Surely Joy will want to leave after two or three days, itching to go back to what she calls her "life's work."

"Life," said Joy to her friend Asta, Charles and Vee's mother. "That's an apt expression."

Kingston is in fog, and from their angle they can only see two kinds of grey — charcoal and feather — where water meets shore.

Tangy sweat floats off Charles. They've only been here

for two days, having crossed over after the end of the school year, yet his skin is already brown. Beauty marks are constellations on the whole of his back.

"Okay," says Sonya. "Let's try."

SONYA HAD BEEN PACKING when her mom came into her room. She had Cyndi Lauper playing on a tape deck that Charles and Vee's parents had given her for Christmas, which, unlike Sonya, they celebrate. Joy turned the sound down and sat down on the edge of her daughter's bed, her small frame dipping the mattress only by a quarter inch. "Did you stay as long as that last year?"

Sonya picked up a shirt that had slid off the bed. "It's the same every year."

"I was thinking you might want to see your friends here instead."

"What friends?"

Her mom didn't touch that, of course. As usual she couldn't take what was actually going on in Sonya's head. Maybe that's because what's going on in Joy's head fills it up to the brim, leaving no room for anything else. A distant cousin once told Sonya that the Holocaust leaks into everything. Which made no sense to Sonya because Joy didn't actually go through the war; Bubby and Zaide did, over forty years ago.

"Asta and Arnold might want to be with their kids. As a family, I mean."

"They don't mind." Sonya didn't put the shirt into her suitcase.

She knows this because she has overheard things. At the Remingtons' cottage, she often tiptoes on the landing and leans over the upstairs banister; one time last year, she heard Vee complain to Asta about an extra place setting. "Why does she have to be here all the time?" she said. Vee was eleven years old then, and thought she could still get away with whining. But that time, Asta sent her to her room and called Sonya down to help her set the table.

Sonya hopes that her mother won't keep her from going. She knows she loves her mother, for sometimes, alone in her bed, she cries about Joy, with only a vague sense of what lies at the root of her grief. But every time she goes to the Remingtons' house, she feels relieved, as if she can breathe again.

"I won't stop you," Joy said as she left the room. In her voice were two things: sadness, probably because Sonya was leaving her again; and a twangy cord of anticipation that meant she was already thinking of whatever task she had planned for her latest project. She spends most of her hours in the attic, surrounded by large canvases, the smell of turpentine, and the sounds of Beethoven from an old tape deck.

EACH SUMMER THE REMINGTONS have a family venture, and each summer Sonya joins them. Last year they'd built a shed. At first, as she handed Arnold Remington a nail gun and helped Charles and Vee carry lumber, she imagined she was being kept occupied so she could feel included. By the end of the summer, though, she was climbing up on the roof and shooting nails into the shingles, all under Arnold's approving eye. Arnold is originally American. He left his parents and siblings when he was young, under circumstances that nobody talks about. He is something she has overheard adults say is a rare thing: an academic who is also a handyman. He believes that children should be self-sufficient, and that every one of them should learn useful, even dangerous skills.

THE ISLAND, SONYA LOVES. The long grasses, the wild-flowers, the dandelion puffs. The Queen Anne's lace and the purple loosestrife. When they were younger they played hide and seek in the grasses, holding in their pee until they couldn't, running to the outhouse a few metres from the cottage. The outhouse was papered with the covers of old *New Yorkers*. Compared to Joy's books on Bosch and Kokoschka and Picasso, the *New Yorker* cartoons seemed silly, even though she understood none of the jokes.

Charles and Vee have always taught her things, and it is Charles who takes the lead. When she was eight, he tried to take the training wheels off her bike so she could learn to ride for real, though he couldn't manage the bolts and had to call his dad. In the end, he and Arnold pushed her off on her bike, and she cycled a good few metres before falling.

Now they stand on the sloping rocky shore a few hundred metres from the cottage. This is where they will practice.

"You'll have to go in for real," Charles jokes. "Not like last year."

"I did!"

"More or less."

The point where the lake water meets her calves seems to her to be a threshold. Above the water, her legs are unmasked in the sun. When she steps down, her feet stir up silt and disappear.

"If you swim the distance from here to the rock over there," says Charles, "you'll know you can circumnavigate the island."

"Pardon?"

"Go around."

She slips in further. The water rises to her neck like a cold glove.

She tries to remember the front crawl she learned long ago in the overcrowded community pool where she took swimming lessons. She kicks away from the shore and executes a few strokes. Her limbs start to ache almost immediately.

He calls out to her. "Don't slam your hands in the water. Bring them down on the knife-edge and stretch them out. You'll glide forward."

She gets tired halfway to the rock and treads slowly, trying not to extend her legs too far down to whatever grows up from the bottom. She turns around so she can see the shore.

Behind the cottage, on rich green grass, Asta sits on a beach chair and reads a murder mystery. Unlike Asta, Joy doesn't rest. Joy is always standing up, painting. When she eats, she sits only as long as it takes to shovel some food into her mouth before going back to work. Sonya has only seen her prone after she's been up all night, working. Then, she sits on the paint-splattered floor of the attic, her legs in a loose cobweb pose. When Sonya found her like that one morning, Joy smiled sadly at Sonya and said something she didn't understand at all. "I'm not even sure I should be *trying* to get this right. A spotlight on evil. I don't know what I'm doing."

Still in the water, Sonya wishes Asta would look up from her book and tell her to come back, that she doesn't have to do this ridiculous swim. She would actually say "ridiculous," for she uses the same words as her husband. Instead, she sits, her short, dirty-blonde hair spiky from an early morning dip. A triangle of sun drapes itself over her left knee. Soon she will move her chair a few inches over so she can stay in the light.

EACH EVENING, AFTER SONYA, Charles, and Vee have put away the dishes, the family goes to the living room. Arnold sits in an armchair and reads a biography of Franklin Roosevelt. Asta leans back into a worn love seat and reads an old *Vogue*. She is originally from Denmark. A long time ago, before she gave up a job to raise her kids, she was a hairdresser or something like it — Sonya knows only that her work involved taking care of women.

The girls are lying on a faded Ikea carpet, painting their nails using Asta's mother-of-pearl polish, their heads almost touching. Vee is teaching Sonya to apply nail polish just so, not quite at the cuticle, so it doesn't spill over.

Books on famous swimmers are scattered on the floor. Naked from his waist up, Charles kneels and puts his hands on either side of a book. He rises on his hands and knees to read the top of a page, his back arching like a bridge. "Who could beat this kind of time?"

"Charles wants to be Kutral Ramesh," Vee says. Ramesh is the youngest person to swim the English Channel.

Asta looks up to gauge which way the conversation is going, to see if Vee is picking a fight. Vee finds her brother annoying. In the water, Vee is as quick and light as a skating bug. It irritates her that her brother always beats her in races. "Ramesh was thirteen. Charles is too old."

"Vee," Asta warns.

Arnold glances at Vee. "When you are as hardworking, you may tease your brother."

Vee blushes and concentrates harder on applying nail polish to her smallest toe.

THROUGHOUT JULY, THEY PRACTISE twice a day. Vee is always the first one in, tiptoeing on the rocks as if they are too hot to linger on, then sliding in. Charles moves slowly but efficiently. Sonya is the last one in, and only after a good minute or two of stalling by pretending to adjust her bathing suit. The suit is one of Vee's old ones. Asta gave it to her after seeing Sonya shiver in her own. She had only brought one bathing suit, which she had to wear while it was still wet from the day before.

Each day, Sonya increases the number of lengths she

swims by almost one. Some days her muscles ache and twice Charles tells her to take an afternoon off. "Your muscles need recovery time." After each day of rest, she swims further than ever before. By August, she can swim fifty lengths. The water is no longer frightening. With each stroke she creates a wall between herself and things that lurk.

One day, she catches her reflection in the mirror of the room she shares with Vee. Her fingers are long and brown, her fingernails are smooth as beach stones. At home, she's often trying to figure things out — how to interrupt Joy's work to ask her to sign a permission slip; what they will eat for dinner, and whether mac-and-cheese two nights in a row will give her a stomach ache — and she's in the habit of biting her cuticles while she thinks. On the island, she hasn't bitten them once.

Sometimes, when Sonya gets home from school, Joy surprises her by being in the kitchen, frying chicken breasts or stirring a bubbling soup on the stove. On those evenings, she plays a card game of war with Sonya. There are moments when, caught in a flurry of card moves, she laughs, and Sonya studies her mother's face, unused to seeing it so happy. Seconds later, her mother frowns. "I forget," she'll say. "What does the joker do in this game anyway?"

When Sonya turns and studies herself in the Remingtons' mirror, she sees that her upper back has developed muscle. She is beginning to resemble, not Vee who is lithe like her father, but Asta and Charles, whose large-boned Scandinavian bodies give off an impression of reliability.

NEIGHBOURS, JEAN AND DAVID Thomas, are expected for dinner. Everybody knows them: five years before, their daughter was the youngest person to swim around the island.

To host them, Asta wears an old Sixties-style dress with enormous flowers. When she appears at the living room door, Arnold says, "That's a bright piece."

Asta frowns. She makes Sonya think of a piece of yellow glass polished by the sea. So unlike Joy, who is so thin she almost disappears. Whenever Sonya makes dinner for Joy, Joy says, "God! If it weren't for you, I'd forget to eat!"

Jean Thomas is a compact woman with blunt fingernails who wears a blue anorak at dinner. Their daughter isn't with them, she explains — she is on a sailing trip for exceptional teenagers. "Ah yes," she says when introduced to Sonya, "the daughter of the artist." Mrs. Thomas keeps each food item separate on her plate.

She peers down her long nose at Sonya. "And what tradition does she work in?"

Sonya tries to remember the words people use to describe her mother's work. Broad strokes in navy and brick red. Skeletal faces whose black pupils almost fill the whites of the eyes. Those canvases that her mother tried to hide by putting them deep into an attic crawlspace. For a moment, the feeling of dread she experiences whenever she sees Joy's paintings obliterates her thoughts. "Reality?" she asks.

"Joy has a growing reputation," says Arnold. "She is a descendant of survivors. What the Jews call the *Shoah*."

"I always forget that you're a historian," Mrs. Thomas says.

"I wonder, though, if there's anything else to say about the Holocaust."

Sonya sees herself as a tiny figure pummelling Mrs. Thomas's face, which is as dense as an acorn. Words fly within her mind like mosquitos and she has trouble choosing which ones to put to Mrs. Thomas. It's always like this, not finding the thing that fits, not being able to defend her mother when people say things about her.

"A resurgence," Arnold says. "Spiegelman puts a spin on it. Cathartic, I would think."

"If someone is saying something more about it, then there's more to say," says Asta.

"Well." Mrs. Thomas picks up her fork and tidies pork chop bundles into her mouth.

Sonya wants to hug Asta, for being on her side. She also wants to hide from her, for she is ashamed of what Asta knows. Asta knows about Joy's big sister. But can she be called a sister when Joy never met her? When she died before Joy was born, even before Zaide was married to Bubby? Sonya turns this question over and over, even while she knows that this question isn't the important one. When she was little, her mother said, "You should know this. I won't do with you what my parents did to me." Sonya doesn't remember the exact conversation, just those words, floating on dark lake water.

Asta once asked Joy, "You haven't shown her that painting, have you?"

Sonya tried to decide which canvas they were talking about,

and whether it had been one of the ones in the crawlspace.

"No," her mother's voice answered.

"I should hope not. There's a limit," said Asta.

But what was the limit? Sonya wondered. And how did you paint one?

JOY PAINTS IN A tradition she calls expressionist, figures bent over or broken, all suffering in some way. Sometimes she paints over them in bursts of red and yellow and fiery orange until almost nothing is left, only a pinprick of black or grey, a cut-off shin or bone. One day, she says to Asta, she will suffuse the canvas with light and it will take over everything.

Sometimes she tells her art dealer over the phone that her latest paintings didn't work out.

"I tried for O'Keefe and ended up with flowers painted by Bosch. Horrifying."

Those paintings, which were spread around the studio for a few weeks last fall, were of enormous flowers — red poppies mostly. The flowers were menacing; Sonya didn't want to stay in the room with them. Joy said, "nobody wants these hanging in their living room." Sonya agreed.

Just before summer, Sonya overheard Asta and Joy talking over tea. Joy was saying, "You don't know what it was like. My dad and his moods. He used to shut himself up in his office with his war journals. When Sonya came along, he either ignored her or wouldn't let her out of his sight. Just like when I was a kid."

Sonya remembers her Zaide helping her cross the street, and her telling him that he didn't really need to do that, that she'd been going to Charles and Vee's house by herself since grade one. Zaide standing on their porch, his gaze a spotlight on her. Although her mother was supposedly somewhere in the house, Sonya could feel her presence, shadowing her Zaide but keeping herself hidden behind a curtain so that no-one would know she was watching. "Children should have some independence," she would say to her father, but Sonya wasn't so sure that she believed it.

"Your daughter needs you," Asta said to Joy.

"I know, I know. I get carried away. But I'm getting closer. I finally figured out the painting had to be from the perspective of the child. A baby who stares at her murderer. Complete ambivalence."

For a split second, Sonya didn't get the word "murderer." Wasn't a soldier just a soldier? But then, a short lesson she'd had in grade seven history, along with the film clips they had seen, came back to her, and she made sense of the word. She waited to see whether her mother would continue speaking and clarify the question, explain what had happened to the child. But her mother didn't say anything more.

"What are you going to do?" Asta asked.

"With Sonya? She wants to be with you this summer. As usual."

"Oh, Joy. If you want her home. But what I meant was, with your work."

"It's really progressing. But no, she should go. I'll keep

at it," Joy said. "It's for Sonya, you know. Maybe after this summer, we can leave it behind. We can live more lightly, you see."

At the start of the summer Joy painted all night, every night. Her eyes were red-rimmed; much of the time, she looked anywhere but at Sonya. Her eyes flitted this way and that, Starlings fluttering from one tree to another. She alternated between ignoring Sonya and bringing her close, embracing her until Sonya's bones felt brittle and her arms sore. For a rare moment, while in her mother's company, Sonya was afraid both for her and of her. She was glad to leave her mother for the Remingtons, who, even-tempered, neither overlook nor smother her.

SONYA AND VEE SUNTAN on the shore that faces away from Kingston. Here there are no cottages, only the rustle of grass, the crackling of pines, and the occasional rumble of a motorboat.

They close their eyes against the sun. Vee wears a purple bathing suit. She is on her back, her budding breasts thrust toward the sky. Sonya lies on her stomach with her head turned and her chest up against the bed of the warm stone.

"Have you kissed anyone yet?" Vee asks.

Sonya opens her eyes. "Have you?"

"There's a guy I'm supposed to go out with when I get back to the city."

"I'm saving myself," Sonya says, then regrets it.

Vee props herself up. "For who?"

Sonya shuts her eyes.

"It's not my brother, is it? Gross."

The light under Sonya's squeezed eyelids goes from yellow to red-black. In the distance, a motorboat approaches, a hum getting louder.

When they return to the cottage, Asta is leaning over an open oven. The kitchen is filled with the scent of roasting chicken. "Your mother called," she says. Asta doesn't have a phone; none of the islanders do. The only phone on the island is located at its centre, in a hut. "Jean Thomas was on the main path when she heard the phone ring," says Asta. She takes a baster to a trussed chicken and curtains its skin with juices. Rising, she says, "There's a flashlight by the door. And take a quarter for the phone."

When Sonya sets out, it's already dark. Her flashlight creates a small, full moon on the dirt path before her. In her periphery, giant pines sway.

The small hut, lit by a naked bulb hanging from the ceiling, is comforting until she catches sight of the spider webs and cobwebs netted up and down its corners. Her coin clatters within the phone's belly.

Joy answers after several rings, her voice sounding far away at first.

"Why are you calling me?" asks Sonya.

"I'm just checking in on you," says Joy.

"Oh."

"Listen. I think I've figured some things out."

Sonya strains her ears for Beethoven. "Are you calling me

because you're on a break?" This is how it usually is: the pity she feels for her mother when they are apart evaporates in her presence.

"No, honey. I just thought. If you wanted to come home."

"Everything's fine." She longs to be back in Asta's kitchen, its warmth and its scent of roasting poultry.

"Right." As usual, Joy gives in to Sonya. If only she persisted, if only she tried to get more out of her daughter, something might change between them. This conversation is no different from those before it, after all.

"I have to get going," says Sonya.

THE NEXT DAY, SONYA has trouble keeping her eyes open in the morning light that filters through the opening in the bedroom curtains. Her nose is runny and her throat sore. Asta brings her ginger ale and feels her forehead. "Stay right here." Sonya is thrilled to have Asta's attention, to give herself over to Asta's care. In this instance, Asta has not disappointed her. Sonya sinks into the sagging mattress and burrows herself under the wool blanket, becoming so hot that she sweats.

Charles comes in later that morning. "You missed practice."

"I'm sick." Her neck is stiff and aches.

"Okay." He shrugs.

She spends the next hour thinking of him swimming, his shoulders flashing above the water. She drags herself out of bed and puts on her bathing suit. The rough grass down to the shore pricks her bare feet.

Charles is sitting on a rock facing the lake. He looks up. "Ah. Great."

"Where's Vee?"

He points to a figure farther along the shore, in the water. "She's moody, as usual."

The cold water takes Sonya's breath away, so she treads quickly to get used to the temperature, as Charles has taught her. After a minute she feels her limbs warm up and loosen. She kicks out, concentrates on technique: rotate arms, kick strong, breathe efficiently. Soon, her body relaxes, glides forward with less effort. She sees herself as if from above, a sea creature with water streaming down its oiled back.

Afterward, she's breathless, aching. The soreness returns, coats the inside of her throat. Charles hands her a towel. "You see? You have to push through."

ACROSS CHARLES'S RIGHT SHOULDER, descending diagonally across his back, is a red welt. After morning practice, he took a canoe out and balanced on the stern, bouncing up and down to move the canoe forward. The islanders call this "gunny jumping." As he tried to walk on the gunwale — like a tightrope walker, imagines Sonya — a motorboat wake unbalanced him and he struck his back on the gunwale's hard edge.

At dinner, Arnold says, "It wasn't smart. You'll need two or three days at least."

"It could have been worse," says Asta.

"He certainly won't do it again."

Charles eats, his nape flushing.

After dinner, Sonya goes to Charles's room. The room has a desk, a single bed, and a shelf, all wood. Charles is seated with his back to her. His legs, too big to fit under what must be a child's desk, are splayed on either side of the chair. A lamp casts a pool of light on some papers. As Sonya approaches, he starts. "What's up?" He covers the papers, then reveals them when he sees it's her.

They are drawings of warships, in delicate blue ink.

"Those are amazing," she says.

"That's the Achilles. From the first ship battle in double u double u two."

She leans over him.

"And here is HMS Prince of Wales. Because of her, the German KMS Bismarck sank." He looks at her. "I'm sorry. I shouldn't talk about the war."

"Oh, it's not the same. Well, I guess it is."

"Does your mother talk about it?"

"Not much."

"Is it true that her older sister was killed in a concentration camp?"

"Yes."

"Do you know how?"

"Well, I —"

"If you don't want to talk about it," he says.

How she wishes she could talk to him, but where could she start?

"Her name was Sonya." Unbidden, tears come to her eyes.

"Forget it." Absentmindedly, he brings his arm around to his back.

"Don't!"

It's too late: he has scratched the sore. He grimaces. "Shit." He picks up a pen and weaves it between his fingers. "What?"

"Nothing."

He pushes his chair out from the desk. "Anyway, I might pass on the swim."

She steadies herself with her hand on the bed. "But you worked so much."

"It might be nice to slack off. My dad —"

"He's pretty scary."

He laughs. "He doesn't scare me. He annoys me." He looks at her. "You're lucky to avoid all this. Family."

Her voice whispering now. "I thought I might follow you. I mean, you know what I mean."

A look that she can't read crosses his face. "Yeah. I know."

ON THE DAY OF the swim, the sky is blue. They go out to the grass above the shore. Asta is at the starting point, seated in her lawn chair. Arnold, who will paddle beside them in the canoe, stands beside his son. He puts his arm around Charles and pulls him into his embrace. "You'll hold up."

Charles smiles shyly and returns his dad's pat on the back. A few seconds later, he starts to jog on the spot. He looks a little silly, like he's in a 1930s Olympic film, one that makes the athletes' movements robotic.

Sonya searches for signs that he's going to change his mind

again. Standing there with a towel around her midsection, she looks out at the water that is cold and black and impenetrable and maybe something that can be tamed, if only temporarily.

"He's concentrating." Vee has come up beside her, wearing a navy blue and white suit that she bought when she got her bronze cross. "Don't bother him."

"I wasn't."

"He has a girlfriend, back at school."

"You're not his boss."

"He doesn't like you," Vee whispers. "He feels sorry for you." She walks away, the scoop of her bathing suit showing off her thin, tough back.

When Sonya finally drops her towel to the grass and moves toward the shore, Vee and Charles are already in the water. There's a cool edge to the wind and the hairs on her upper arms rise. She stands on a rock and lets the water lap her toes. She is thinking of how, when push comes to shove, the Remingtons help one another, stick together as a family.

For a moment Sonya forgets what comes next. Her calves strain like a dog on a leash, but her feet grip the rock. As if, in going in, she risks everything: her family, herself. The swim, like all the things Sonya does with the Remingtons, separates Sonya from her mother. Standing there, she feels, behind her rib cage, a languid caress of guilt.

Sonya pictures her arms windmilling, pushing aside things that give shape to horror and grief. Driving them down to the silt-covered bottom of the lake.

Vee and Charles tread water a few metres away. Charles

puts his hands around his mouth. His voice arcs over the expanse. "Are you coming?"

Starting Somewhere

MY CABIN WAS ONE of ten scattered up a hill like a flight of steps. Each one housed ten campers and two counsellors. The buildings had been refinished and I could still smell the addictive scent of wood stain. The screen doors were rickety and their hinges squeaked. None of them shut properly: I had to pull hard to get the latch to click.

Each evening, my co-counsellor Jen and I sat on our steps, with Darren joining us. He sprawled at our feet against the bottom step, and complained — mostly about me.

"Lyds showed me a naked chick today." He grinned, but his face was red.

"I was giving a camper a shower." We were supposed to call them clients, but I couldn't wrap my head around it. "You walked in."

This wasn't strictly true. I'd told him to come in, and he had.

The camper, Betty Bernowski, was in her fifties. Like the others, she had a disability — something genetic, I think. She'd stood under the water with her eyes closed, and I couldn't tell if she was loving the water or feeling trapped by it; just biding her time until I told her to come out. Betty was overweight and her buttocks seemed to overflow onto the backs of her thighs. Covering both buttocks was a large mark consisting of two concentric circles, one inside the other.

Darren shrugged. "You could have warned me."

He was fifteen, a virgin, and he liked me. At home, I was having a bad time with the girls at school. I'd slept with most of the eleventh grade guys, but had no real girlfriends. Teasing Darren felt like a sort of escape valve.

"And thanks for the little present," he added. Betty was in the shower because she had soiled herself on the bench outside the dining room, and I'd left the mess for him.

"That's your job," I said. It came out a little shaky.

"Is seeing someone naked wrong?" Jen said. "Fundamentally, I mean." It always gave me a jolt, seeing someone with hair the colour of her purple consider things seriously.

"Wouldn't you care?" Darren said.

"No." Jen tugged at her tank top and made as if to flash him. "Get the frig out of here."

I could do it, I thought. I could pretend that my body meant nothing more than a collection of skin cells, that my nipples were just tagged-on conglomerations.

"We shouldn't be so hung up on nakedness. I mean, we're all the same. Society has to start somewhere. Why not with our campers?" Jen got up. "I need repellent."

The screen door, set up to protect campers' fingers, shut slowly. Looking into the cabin from the porch, I could see a row of bathroom sinks at the far end. To the left, out of sight, were bunk beds. Our small alcove bedroom was on the immediate right as I walked in; it had an accordion door that, like the front door, didn't close well, always bouncing back with a gasp and leaving a two-inch gap, which made me feel a perpetual lack of privacy.

Jen, Darren, and I were at the camp for more or less the same reasons. I'd come to get away from my mom and make money for clothes. Jen, who was from The Kingsway, in western Toronto known for its hundred-year-old trees and six-bathroom houses, was probably there for a similar purpose. Darren was definitely in it for the cash: he once wore the same *Star Trek* T-shirt three days in a row, and only changed when Jen complained about the smell.

Other counsellors saw their jobs as preludes to their social work careers. Jen called them "do-gooders." She especially disliked Murray, our camp director. When Murray hired me, he'd asked me to rate my desire to work at the camp on a scale of one to ten. He liked formulas.

I'd smiled sweetly. "Nine-point-five."

"Perfect." And he unfolded his body — he was over six feet — from behind his desk to shake my hand.

Whenever Jen saw Murray around camp, overseeing

camper activities, she'd whisper, "Is Murray putting on his director's face again?"

He really did look like he was only pretending to care, with his gesticulating hands, his ever-widening blue eyes, and his Saint Bernard jowls.

When they'd first come off the camp bus, the campers had shouted out greetings and hugged counsellors they had known for years. To someone like me, who had never paid attention to people with special needs, their differences stood out. Their eyes seemed either too deep-set, or bulging. Their lips appeared narrow or bulbous and wet. Above all, they were noisy. Many of them yelled when they spoke. It was as if they knew they wouldn't be heard unless they made themselves louder than everyone else. I saw they could be divided into two categories: boisterous or withdrawn. The quiet campers tended to stare. Betty Bernowski was a starer. Her look held no judgment, though, which killed me; the world needed people to take a stance.

The camp ran itself. Each day, we walked the campers to their assigned places: the dining hall, the art barn, the music room, the swimming beach. Like herding cattle, I thought on my bad days. Back then, I was callous, and didn't always think of them as real people. Still, we had responsibilities. On the first day, Murray had taken us out onto the open grass down the hill from the dining hall to give us instructions. He'd talked about how the campers sometimes snuck out of their cabins at night to have sex. "They have natural urges," he'd said. "But we don't encourage it."

"He's a hypocrite," Jen hissed afterwards. "Didn't he just lecture us on the importance of autonomy?" Her nose ring refracted the sunlight. "They have a right to their bodies."

I loved Jen. She really didn't give a damn about what anyone thought of her.

LOGAN DIDN'T LOOK LIKE a lifeguard. He was skinny and had a white guy's afro and wore synthetic shorts through which you could see the details of his bulge. He didn't seem to notice, just paraded around the camp, sometimes stopping to talk to someone, one hand on his thrust-out hip like a girl. Because he'd been returning to camp for several years, he did what he wanted. Often he could be found at the camp docks, smoking a cigarette, preparing himself for his shift.

"He's taken," Jen told me. "Michelle."

"Seriously? She's so —"

"Obviously a catch?" Darren said.

"Do you think she gives him what he needs?"

"She's got that classic look," Jen said. "Blonde."

"Maybe he wants something more exotic."

"I don't think he's ready," Jen said.

"He's not that special," Darren added.

Once a week, each of us had night patrol. Patrollers were supposed to check in on the campers, but, since Jen had once told me I was too conscientious, I no longer went into each cabin to sweep my flashlight over sleeping faces. I simply listened at doors.

One night, sounds came from Michelle's cabin. I knew that

she was out that night, probably by the docks with Logan. Her campers should have been asleep. I stepped closer. The cry from within came again, its meaning unmistakable now. I peered behind me, on the lookout for Murray, who liked to make his own rounds. Every night, he walked up and down the path parallel to the cabins, flashing a torch flashlight and humming a tune from *Guys and Dolls*. Tonight, Murray wasn't in sight, and I walked back down the hill without going into Michelle's cabin.

Jen sat on her cot in our room, painting her nails violet. "What's wrong?"

I told her what I'd heard.

"Can you imagine if Michelle walks in on them," she said.

"Would she even know what it is?"

ONE WEDNESDAY, WE RAN all the way to the camp gates and farther still, gravel pockmarking our bare legs, pine-scent rushing up our nostrils. We ran as if someone were after us, as if Murray would suddenly appear and say, "What, guys, is it your day off or something? And I thought you actually liked it here."

Darren led us through trailer park gates and then to a trailer. A sign on the door of the trailer read, *Welcome to Our Home*.

Jen stood still. "Is this a joke?"

Darren smiled lopsidedly and took out a key.

We walked into a kitchen. Beside a sink, a squat tap gleamed. A washcloth folded in quarters was draped over an empty drainer, which sat on a white counter. There was a little white fold-out table. A yellow, floral curtain fluttered over a small window.

Darren opened a tiny fridge, the kind my dad had in the garage to stock for summer parties. He took out three beers, then led us to the back of the trailer, into his bedroom, and handed one to each of us. He lifted his beer. "To freedom."

We sat on his single bed, our backs knocking the particle board wall, our feet dangling over the edge of the mattress. Jen's leg touched mine, which as usual she didn't notice: she had no idea what personal space was. I didn't mind, though. Not like those girls at school who would shriek if I so much as skimmed them in the halls with my knapsack.

The bedroom window was open. A faint smell of gasoline, latrine, and gardenias hung in the air. Apart from occasional shouts of children, there was a far-off drone of a highway, and a steady chirp of crickets. In between these small noises, the quiet thrummed. Back home, whenever I took a minute to myself on our back deck, my mom would come out and nag me to do some chore. Like she was waiting to pounce.

"You're lucky." Alcohol spread up from my abdomen and into my chest, which made me feel both very happy and very sad. "Don't your parents mind?"

Darren shrugged. "My booze, my rules."

"Are they even here?" Jen asked.

"My mom works double shifts at a diner up the road." He swigged his beer. "Anyway, one more year and I'm outta here."

"And you're off to ...?" Jen asked.

"Secretarial college in TO. There are a lot of jobs." He stared hard at us.

"We're not laughing," Jen said.

Darren's leg fell against mine. "Yup," he said. "Rent is taken care of. The camp job will pay for the books. One more year and I'm set." He frowned.

He tuned a transistor radio until he hit on Guns N' Roses. Then he sat back down. His leg bounced to the music. With each movement, his jeans rubbed against my bare right knee.

When Jen got up to use a washroom that, despite being on the other side of the trailer, seemed too close, Darren rose to turn up the music. "You know." He winked. "To cover up."

Later, he gathered our empties, opened a cupboard under the kitchen sink, and slotted them into their case. With a dishrag, he wiped the wet bottle rings off the counter.

SOMEONE MUST HAVE SAID something to Murray about what happened in Michelle's cabin. The next day, I came out of the main building's bathroom, into the lobby, to find Murray and Michelle talking. They stood near a wall that was tiled in yellow; the colour appeared to extend from Michelle's hair to form several bright sun rays around her head.

Murray bent over her. "I understand one of your campers was intimate with another."

She looked down. On her cheeks were two round spots.

"Have you thought that someone might get pregnant?" he asked.

"Betty is old —"

"Extrapolate, please, Michelle. It's our job to keep our campers safe."

In the end he patted her arm and let her go. As I left the lobby, Logan came through the door to the dining hall and drew Michelle in for a hug.

I FIGURED THAT LOGAN just needed time to get to know me. After all, guys had never been a problem. One day, I followed him to the lakefront. The swimming area was cordoned off on two sides. Perpendicular to the shore was an L-shaped, light-blue dock, which swayed in the wind.

Logan paced on the dock and smoked. There was a morning swim and an afternoon swim, and he smoked before and after each one.

When the dock trembled, he looked up.

I moved forward. "Can I bum a cigarette off you?"

"Sorry, all out."

"I'm Lydia, by the way." I held out my hand.

He stared at it. "I know who you are."

I nodded. What was it with this one?

"You from that high school in the city? Meadowvale or Sunnyvale?" he asked.

"Meadowvale. How did you know?"

"Every year, they send us some."

"It's a good opportunity."

He snorted.

"What?"

"Forget it." He threw his cigarette into the water, where it floated like a bit of ribbon. He turned toward the shore.

"No, really." I smiled in a way I considered winning.

He spun around. "Here's the thing. You don't know what you're doing."

"I know enough —"

"Really. Did you know that Betty Bernowski was abused?"

"I didn't know if it was true," I said.

"What about those burn marks on her backside? Someone sat her down on a stove when she was a kid."

I stared. "Oh my God. I didn't realize."

"Right. People like you. Campers suffer because of you." He turned away again.

"Don't you mean 'clients'?"

"What?" He glanced at me out of his periphery.

"Clients!" I shouted. "We're supposed to call them clients. It's politically correct."

He marched back. "I could draw circles around you, girl."

I WENT OUT INTO the woods. Just took off right after lunch. I figured the post-lunch nap-time would last an hour. Jen could handle the cabin while I was out. I needed to get out of there. The messes, the noise, Logan — I'd had enough.

He knows nothing about me, I thought. Nothing at all.

The path started in the woods, but almost immediately opened up into a field. The grass was beige in spots. My body moved through floating wisps of milkweed. Soon, the path went past an apple orchard, and the scent of baked apples joined that of dry grass. The sun fell on my shoulders. I picked up the pace.

After a while I felt better. *I'll stick it out*, I decided. The money, at least, was worth it.

I was halfway around a loop that we had hiked as a camp group two weeks before. It didn't make sense to backtrack, so I went around the loop. The path went through fields, then woods again, before circling back to a different part of the camp, near the water. When I broke out of the woods, my legs were scratched from nettles. I saw from my wristwatch that I had been away for two hours instead of one. Nap time had ended, and swim period had come and gone. A breeze hit the sweat on my forehead.

Near the swimming beach, beside a large oak, a group of counsellors was gathered. This was weird, for the swimming area itself was empty. Even stranger was the makeup of the group: Michelle, Logan, Murray, and Jen. Jen didn't like any of those guys. Who was with our campers?

Jen sat on a log under the oak, her head in her hands. Michelle was beside her.

When I was a few meters away from them, Murray and Logan looked up.

"We have a situation, here, Lydia," Murray said.

"Jen, what's wrong?" I asked.

She looked up. Her eyelashes were wet. "It was a bit too much."

"What happened is that you didn't do your job," Murray said.

"Logan saved a camper from drowning," Michelle said. "The others freaked. Jen couldn't deal with them. No offence, Jen."

"You know how it is, Lyds," Jen said. "They feel what's going on around them."

"You saved someone?" I asked Logan.

Michelle answered. "He saw someone floating. And he just went in."

Logan looked bewildered. "I just did it. Without thinking, you know?" He took out a cigarette. I expected someone to stop him, but no one did. When he lit up, his hands shook.

"Where were you?" Murray asked me.

"Walking. Just needed to recharge."

"How many campers do you have?"

"What do you mean?"

"How many?"

"Ten."

"Jen had ten campers on her own, while you went traipsing about."

Logan narrowed his eyes at me. "I heard that you were on patrol duty the night Betty was caught in *flagrante*."

"*Delícto*," I said. "It's in *flagrante delícto*." I couldn't help it. I was always a bit of a snob. Another reason most girls hated me, I suppose.

"You should kick her out," Logan said.

"Now." Murray made an appeasing gesture. "You did well today, but I'm still the boss."

"I'm sorry," I said to Jen.

"Lydia, go up to your cabin and take over from Shelley," Murray said.

"The secretary?"

"Tonight, after Jen has rested, she can watch the cabin and I'll see you in my office."

"I'm going to lie down," Jen said.

"I'll go with you." Michelle put an arm around Jen. They walked away like that, together, all the way up the hill.

JEN STAYED IN BED until after dinner, leaving me in charge of bringing the campers down to the dining hall and then back up the hill to bed, which meant that after I'd undressed everyone and tucked them in, I'd wanted to scream to all of them to get the frig to bed already. And I still needed to talk to Murray.

It was dark by the time I came back from Murray's office. Darren was sitting on the front steps of our cabin.

"How did it go?" he asked.

"He can talk."

"Yeah."

"He expects more from me, and he thinks he sees maturity."

"Phew."

I looked at him.

"I thought he would fire you," said Darren.

"Yeah, well." I was too embarrassed to tell him that Murray had put me on probation, that one more step in the wrong direction would get me kicked out. I pictured telling my parents. My father would say, "There's a lesson here." My mother's eyes would glint in a way that meant, triumphantly, "I told you so." She too had warned me repeatedly about my irresponsibility.

"Where's Jen?" I asked.

"She went out. Said she needed fresh air."

"She left you here with the campers?"

"Wait. Are you complaining about that?"

I sat on the steps. Automatically, I checked for wood-stain marks on my shorts, even though the wood had been dry for weeks.

"What kills me," I said, "is she's always telling me to think for myself."

"But she's your friend."

I slapped a mosquito on my thigh and wiped away the blood with my finger. After a while I asked him if he wanted to go inside.

He looked surprised. "Sure."

Darren held the screen door open for me. I went into the alcove bedroom. Moonlight filtered through the open window, so I kept the light off, and reached behind him to close the door. It bounced back, leaving a one-inch gap.

"Forget it," I said when he made a move to close it again. "It never works. Lie down."

"Why?"

"Do you want a massage?"

"I won't say no." His voice had risen by half an octave.

"Take off your shirt."

He took it off quickly and threw himself on my cot.

I straddled him and went to work.

"Hmmm." His eyes were closed.

I took off my shirt and leaned into his skin.

"Oh," he said.

Was this all there was? Yet being in control felt good. It was like with all those other boys, a taut line of power, a deep thrill that ignored consequences.

The light came on, and I flew off.

Betty stood in the doorway, her square, middle-aged face contemplating us. A look between curiosity and amusement crossed her face. I had this strange urge to flaunt everything, to bare the rest of myself to her.

Murray's head rose behind her right shoulder. He must have been on his rounds. "What the hell." He bent his neck to fit under the doorframe. A giraffe. A giggle struggled to loose itself from my throat. "You, out," he said to Darren.

Darren picked up his shirt and moved toward the door.

"Pack your bags. You can take the bus into the city tomorrow."

Darren stared at Murray. "But I live here. I mean, just outside camp." He had that goofy grin he got whenever he was nervous.

"As long as you're out by morning."

Darren stopped smiling. He looked at me and then at Murray. His eyes went back and forth between us and then settled on me. Red rose into his face, then leached out as he tried to remember why it was that he couldn't be angry at me.

"And you," said Murray, to me. "Do you have any idea how inappropriate this is?"

"Betty is an adult."

"I don't care. You are in a position of power."

We argued some more. He told me I was fired. All the while, I kept my arms where they'd landed when he came through the door: crossed, crushing my T-shirt against my chest.

STAGE PRESENCE

FIVE YEARS BEFORE JESSE died, I ran into him in the shopping centre below my building. I was entering; he was on his way out. He bumped my shoulder, put out a hand as if to steady me, then retracted it. "Amy. What are you doing here?"

"I live upstairs."

"I'm in the next complex! Wait." He reached his hand out again, placing it on my forearm. "I've been wanting to talk to you."

In the fluorescent light, his forehead glistened with sweat, as if it were covered in a layer of plastic wrap. His cheeks were doughy and his red hair no longer shone in the way I remembered. He looked worried. Anxiety was a quality I didn't associate with him. And there was something else, too, which I couldn't place.

"Do you want to come to my party?" I asked.

"I was thinking something quieter."

I hadn't wanted him to come, but now I did. Some old affection had grabbed me. "You'll like my friends. They're from film school."

"So you did it."

Was that envy in his voice?

"I'll come."

JESSE WAS THE FIRST to arrive that evening. He wore a down coat, though he'd only had to walk around the block to get from his apartment to mine.

"Everyone's on their way," I said.

I wanted all my successes to unfold before him. I felt an odd breathlessness, as if I were yearning for the friendship that had been extinct for years.

Jesse was my only friend when I was twelve. He was beautiful, with near-feminine features: that skin Victorian writers described as porcelain, a long narrow nose, and thick reddish curls. I wonder now whether his pallor was due to a chronic kidney illness, which he'd had since childhood. He almost never talked about his poor health, nor about his regular visits to the hospital for dialysis. He joked constantly and it was impossible to have a serious conversation with him. I'd assumed that he felt close to me because we both had absent fathers, until we found our common obsession with movies. He lived with his mother, who worked for an acting agency and had arranged employment for him as a child actor on a historical drama on public television. By the time he reached high school, he needed classes that accommodated his filming schedule, so he chose an alternative school for actors and dancers — and I followed him.

I put Jesse's jacket in my bedroom. "Do you want a drink? Or a tour?"

"I'll take the tour." He moved toward an east-facing window overlooking Toronto's skyscrapers. "Nice view. I face the other side."

"On clear nights you can see the CN Tower. Not to mention the neighbour opposite, who walks around naked."

"Nice." Frost had crept up the window in an arc like a peacock's plumage. Jesse rubbed at it with an index finger.

"Are you sure I can't get you a drink?"

"I can't. My kidneys."

"How is all that?"

He raised his eyebrows. "Alright."

"How about a Perrier?" I said, fleeing into my kitchen.

The year he turned seventeen, his illness had worsened. He was absent from school for an unusually long time, and when he returned, he'd gained weight. His features had softened, as if we were seeing him through an unfocussed camera lens. He wore glasses, oversized frames he must have pulled out of a drawer. *Poor guy*, I'd thought, *he can't wear his contacts*. By that time I'd stopped talking to him, and my pity was coupled with an uneasy justification. Everything we did in those years rode on our appearance and I figured that his marred looks were punishment for his bad behaviour toward me.

Now he wore wire-rimmed glasses, as dated as his first pair.

"I'm going to make a call," I shouted from the kitchen. Although the room was open-concept, the cement dividing wall absorbed sound, and I was forced to raise my voice. I picked up the cordless phone. "Figure out where everyone's at."

AT ONE TIME OR another, we've all thought of high school as a space of possibility. The evening before my daughter started grade nine, she talked about the outfit she would wear, as if by wearing the right thing she could control what would happen to her in the subsequent four years. As if overnight she would become someone other than who she was. Children think they can perpetually make themselves up. They're optimists that way.

My own high school had been filled with kids who were professional artists. Ballerinas and actresses minced into school in preppy clothes, carrying portfolios of their head shots which they giggled over at lunchtime. I understood even then that beauty could propel a person through the world, that behind good looks a person could hide all shortcomings.

Once, I strode into class with my chin up, as if I were balancing a book on my head. "You walk funny, Amy," a ballerina said. She was thin and had short hair like an enormous black brush stroke. "I'm joking! Jesse, tell her I'm joking."

Jesse, sitting at a desk, looked up and smiled gently. "Buck up, Amy," he said. He wasn't interested in teenage girls' dramas.

WHEN MY FRIENDS FINALLY showed up at the party, they tumbled in with the chaos typical of those used to having stage presence. Angus and Christian came in first and shook the snow off their boots.

"Damn, it's cold," Angus said.

Behind them came Angus's girlfriend, who stared at Jesse. "I'm Caterina." She extended her hand, forcing Jesse to cross the room to shake it.

They moved toward my sitting area, two cream-coloured love seats and a couch pushed against a wall. In the middle was a pentagon-shaped, faux-marble table. Caterina and Angus sat kitty-corner rather than beside each other, which made me wonder if today was an off day in their on-again, off-again relationship. Angus, as usual, sprawled, looking as if he took up more space than he actually did. Christian sat opposite him, his self-esteem suffering in Angus's presence. Christian worked hard at school, but no one noticed whereas Angus was inconsistent in his efforts, but when he paid attention he blew everyone away. Passionate about something, he talked fast, leapfrogging from one idea to the next; I could almost see his synapses firing.

Caterina beamed at Jesse, who sat beside her on the sofa between the love seats. She was from Latvia, and had a brashness I've come to recognize in many Eastern European women since then. She had no qualms about tackling things directly. When Angus first introduced her to us, he told us that she was living off her parents, who didn't know their daughter was in film school; they thought she was enrolled in a math program at what we called the "real" university. In response to Angus, who seemed astonished that a person could do such a thing, Caterina nodded calmly. "What they don't know won't hurt them. After all, only I know what is good for me."

She had also made it clear to Angus that she didn't believe in monogamy. He'd admitted this to Christian and me in a drunken moment of intimacy. I admired Caterina's confidence, but felt sorry for Angus and couldn't understand how she could take a guy like him for granted.

Jesse was telling Caterina that he lived next door.

"Nice if you can afford it," Christian said.

"My landlord lives in the States," I said. "He's clueless about rents here."

"My condo's not actually mine," said Jesse.

"Do you have a rich wife?" Caterina laughed.

"It belongs to my ex."

"Really?" I said.

Jesse shrugged. "Life is short."

Girls had liked Jesse, but he'd never had a girlfriend. There were rumours that he was gay, but they were dismissed, and no one could figure out why he didn't date.

I felt a jolt of jealousy, which surprised me, given our history. I got up for more beer.

When I came back, they were talking about Cronenberg's *Naked Lunch*, which had come out in theatres a few weeks before.

"It reminded me of *Eraserhead*," Christian said.

"Yeah," said Angus. "A transgressive masterpiece."

I sat down. "Kind of masturbatory, I thought."

"Yes!" Caterina said. "That giant penis. Oh my God."

"In the end," Jesse said, "it's just a junkie's hallucinations."

Angus looked thoughtfully at Jesse.

Christian said, "You in the movie business?"

"He's an actor," I said. We waited for him to say that he had something lined up. This was an expression we in the film industry knew well. We were competitive (I always wondered whether it was by nature or by nurture. The industry seemed to draw people who were naturally driven, and then nurtured them, through a paucity of work and funding bodies, to become even more cutthroat.) We lived in dread of hearing that someone we knew had something lined up; and were thrilled to make the pronouncement about ourselves, when possible.

"I used to be," Jesse said.

"Speaking of which," Christian said. "Angus, did you tell them?"

Angus swigged his beer. "I got a gig."

"An internship with TVO," said Christian.

"Just for the summer."

"The guy applies for one job and gets it."

Angus shrugged. "It's always been like that."

"Also Amy," Caterina said. "Right?"

"What did Amy do?" Christian asked.

"Won that school prize," said Caterina, "For most beautiful documentary."

"Best cinematography," I corrected her.

Christian raised his glass. "To our two stars." We raised our glasses.

"What was it for?" Jesse asked.

I looked at him. "A small film on the rave scene."

"She spent weeks going to every rave in the city," said Angus.

"All those drugged-up girls," Christian said.

"I was envious," I said, and Angus and Christian laughed. I turned to Jesse. "About the power of the rave. How it re-signifies the female body."

"She went postmodern on us. It was a smart little piece, Amy," Angus said. He wasn't laughing at me anymore. I knew from past conversations with him that he had partly understood what I'd been trying to do with my film, for I had tried to angle the shots in such a way that the ravers' control in the situation was obvious.

"It doesn't surprise me," Jesse said. "We used to make movies together."

"Ah, you are high-school lovebirds!" Caterina smiled.

"No," I said.

AT SIXTEEN, WE SPENT after-school hours in Jesse's mother's lakefront condo, writing scripts and filming them with his video camera. We camped out on his mother's deep couch and passed a notebook back and forth, our wrists brushing. Later that winter, influenced by the French New Wave, we wrote a kind of Canadian version of Jean-Luc Godard's *Breathless*, set in Toronto. Because there were only two of us, we could only have one actor in each shot, and had to film in such a way that a second character's presence was implied.

In one scene, I was required to seduce a male character, played in turn by Jesse. I don't remember the lines. I do remember feeling that I pushed myself aside, reaching within to find the person I wanted to be. Afterward, Jesse stared at me. My cheeks flushed. "I don't know how to describe it. I felt high."

Watching the video, I was shocked at how undressed I looked. My breasts were almost bared, revealing half of a nipple. Yet the camera flattered me. I was skinny, and the lens added much-needed flesh to my body. My face's sharp lines were filled in. I'd always thought I was pretty, and there was the proof. I glanced at Jesse to see if he'd noticed but he said nothing. So I tried to goad him into it. "You won't show this to anyone, right?"

"Yeah. I mean, no."

He popped the videotape out, slotted it back in its case, and put it on a bookshelf. When I came back the following week, the tape was gone.

MORE PEOPLE ARRIVED AT my party en masse, all from the film department, all very noisy and boisterous. Under their thick jackets, the women wore jeans that flattered their asses and tank tops that left their shoulders bare, polished like beach stones. Practically the whole department had showed up, which thrilled me.

I took coats, handed out drinks, and turned up Joy Division

on the stereo. When I came back, Caterina and Angus were having one of their usual arguments.

Caterina was saying, "What I mean, Angie,"— when angry, she pronounced his name with a soft G; I was never sure if she did this on purpose — "is that you are a man, white, and charming. You are in a good position to find work."

"Not in Canada," Angus said.

"You Canadians think you are so advanced, so different from Europe."

"When it comes to looks, girls have the advantage," Christian interjected. "I read that pretty people are three times as likely to be employed as ugly people."

"You see," Caterina said.

"You're full of crap." Angus rose. He was a greyhound impatient for a hunt to get started. "I'm going for a smoke."

"Be careful," I said. "The balcony is slippery."

"I will stay with someone who doesn't get mad." Caterina pushed a beer toward Jesse, who had been watching them argue. He looked slightly amused, as if the argument neither concerned him nor mattered to him very much, which I found surprising; I had been waiting for him to say something. In any case, I was irritated that my friends couldn't put on a better show for him. I wanted him to think that all was perfect in my world, that I was just *fine*, thanks.

"We are not usually so annoying," said Caterina to Jesse. She winked at me. "Well, it is possible that we are."

I retrieved my coat and, without zipping up, went out onto the balcony. It was a tiny space, about three feet deep and six feet wide, with a low cement ceiling. In the summer, my upstairs neighbours' plants dripped on the planter hanging on my railing.

Angus sat on a beach chair, smoking. Both breath and smoke went up in short, cloudy bursts. Beside him was a young woman, one of several first-years at the party. She wore a faux-fur hood, from under which peeked out blonde strands.

"Miranda," Angus said, "This is Amy, our host."

"Is it?" She peered up at me. "Welcome to our balcony."

"Well, thanks." I shivered.

"Have a seat." Angus opened his coat as if to make room for me. "I need someone to warm me up."

I sat down on his lap and leaned back, felt the bristles of the hair on his chest, the ones that came up above his T-shirt. For a moment I was thrilled at the vision of our heads together, my own narrow face beside his equally long one, my thick brown hair caressing his cheek. I pictured him and me, far into the future, crossing the stage together to receive our film accolades.

"How are things with Caterina?" I asked him.

"Caterina is Caterina."

"Are you guys together?"

"Together, apart." He stubbed his cigarette out on the armrest. "She can take care of herself." His breath smelled like ashes.

I went back in, finding it too cold to stay out. Christian was with a crush of others in the kitchen. Caterina and Jesse were still seated. Caterina looked at the porch door and then at me. Her eyes seemed hurt. She turned back to Jesse, who to my surprise had a beer in front of him. He had unbuttoned the top two buttons of his shirt and was sitting with his legs spread out.

"She left me for another guy, but she still drives me to dialysis! What kind of woman does that?" he asked.

"She still has love for you. This is so rare." Caterina stared at me as she said this.

"Maybe you can persuade her to come back." He too turned to me, his eyes wet.

I figured out what I'd sensed in him that morning, in the shopping court, why he was here now. It took me a long time to understand, which was strange — loneliness was something I knew well.

"Maybe Amy could extol my virtues." Jesse drank. "But I don't think so. Amy has held a grudge for years. She has nothing good to say about me."

I blushed. I had never before been confronted about the past in quite that way, with someone presenting it to me like a wrapped package. I dropped onto the armrest of the sofa opposite them. Someone had switched the music to acid house, which thrummed through the couch.

"Amy!" said Caterina loudly, over the music. "How is the ethics committee going?"

"The what?" Jesse asked.

"She filmed those girls on drugs."

"We're working it out," I said.

"They did not sign consent forms, right, Amy?" Caterina's look was steady.

"There weren't any complaints, so school won't pursue it."

"Little girls will not come chasing after you."

"First of all, they're seventeen. Women," I said.

I couldn't tell if she was serious or trying to be mischievous, but I felt myself becoming irritated. I'd discussed the issues with the committee and didn't want to talk to Caterina about it. I was annoyed with her for not being more on Angus's side, when my affection for him was growing. I was also astonished that, given her propensity for self-invention, she didn't understand my film.

I had sat in front of the committee and tried to persuade them that I had meant no harm. They were men and women who had assembled after someone, probably a conservative-leaning parent, had contacted the department. At first, I told the administrators, I thought the ravers were just doing what young women sometimes did, which was to act sexy to get picked up. But as I scrutinized them, I realized that something else was going on. They were not performing at all. I described what I had seen; I even showed the committee some film clips. They were not exploited, I explained. I had tried to capture the women's power with my camera. The committee members had glanced at each other and I thought they had been persuaded. They told me they would get back to me formally, by letter, but I hadn't yet received their verdict.

I didn't want to get into all this with Caterina. And Jesse didn't look sober enough to even begin to understand any kind of explanation I had.

"Excuse me, ladies," Jesse said. He got up and left the room.

Caterina watched him. "He is a sad guy, that friend of yours."

AT THE END OF grade twelve, people started treating me differently. I had never been popular, but now other students seemed to single me out. Girls clumped together, whispering when I walked by, and boys I'd never talked to catcalled me. I didn't understand why until, one day, I was standing beside Jesse in the hallway when someone walking by whispered, "Porn," and Jesse seemed nervous.

I stared at him. "Are you serious?"

"Some of the guys were over, and Alex picked up the tape. You know Alex."

"You let him watch our movie?"

"You looked good, you know. Really good."

"You're such an asshole."

He glared at me. "The movie was your idea."

I FOUND JESSE IN my bedroom looking at prints I had on the wall above my bed. One was a still from Luc Besson's *Nikita*, in which Nikita, her eyes wide with listening intent, crouches with a gun in her hand. The other print was from the original version of *Breathless*, featuring a close-up of Michel, his gun by his thigh, arrested in mid-run, as if he's been shot.

"Similar plots," he said, gesturing to the posters with his chin. "More than that of course. Both directors valued style over narrative."

Now that he mentioned them, their similarities seemed obvious. I saw the two of us on his mother's couch, discussing films as we sat cocooned in the overheated condo while, outside, frozen rain pelted the windows.

"Your friends are interesting," he said. "But a bit nasty, eh?"

"It's a competitive field."

"I guess."

"You had an advantage," I said. "A mother in the business. Plus, you were cute."

He paused. Then he said, "I wanted to say. Since this morning. Since long ago, really. I'm sorry about what happened back then."

"You don't say."

"I bumped into some friends years ago and we talked about it."

I didn't answer right away. I wanted him to repeat his apology, simply because when he'd said it I hadn't felt the way I thought I would. "You talked about me?"

"Sort of. How we were all pretty messed up. I found some others, but I couldn't find you. I tried, though."

"Is this like twelve stages or something?" I asked.

He seemed confused.

"The forgiveness stage. Are these the twelve stages of dying? Like AA?"

He reached for the wall, his fingers fanned out under the photo of Michel.

"Forget it," I said. "Forget I said that."

He found his puffy jacket on the bed under several others. "Let me ask you a question."

My heart was beating. I had an urge to confide in him about the embarrassment and pain I'd suffered back then, but even as several images of my adolescent hurts appeared in my mind's eye, I understood that he would never fully get it.

"You filmed those girls," he said.

It took me a second to reorient my thoughts, for I hadn't been expecting him to bring the subject up, and when I understood what he was talking about, I got angry. True, my movie had won an award, but the naysayers haunted me. I was so damned sick of defending my work. At the same time, I thought, *So he does care about movie making, after all. And he cares about who gets hurt and who inflicts the pain.*

"It's not the same," I said. "I thought you would understand. But maybe you wouldn't, given your history."

"I just apologized. Didn't you hear me?"

"You don't know what you're talking about. These girls, as you call them, were in control of their actions."

In my explanatory piece accompanying my film, I had called them young women, even though they seemed too young to be called anything but girls. And yet, as they danced, they were strong, stronger than I had been at their age. Dressed in silver tops and short skirts, they had loosened their bodies like rag dolls, then tightened them in a kind of ecstasy. In the blinking strobe lights, their limbs had multiplied, and they had made me think of Kali, the ten-armed Indian goddess.

Throughout, they kept their eyes closed, their faces were drawn inward as if they were looking for something that we, as onlookers, were unable to see. They were not performing; they didn't care if anyone — men or women — watched. They could have been alone in their rooms. They made and owned their own pleasures.

With my camera, I focused on their strong, outstretched fingers, their faces that shut everyone out. I did not emphasize their breasts or their bared midriffs. I had tried to change the gaze of the cinematographer and, by doing so, that of the audience. Back in high school, Jesse had filmed me with a masculine vision. If I had loved the version of prettiness he and I had concocted together, it was because I had been socialized to do so — I knew that now, after years of film and political theory. I wanted to film these other girls — these women — from a woman's viewpoint. But perhaps I had not succeeded; didn't the ethics' committee prove this? Suddenly I was devastated by the fresh news of my failed artistic vision.

I wanted to explain all this to Jesse, to tell him that the two movies were made from dissimilar intents and with differing perspectives. I wanted to ask him to watch my film, so he could see how unlike it was to the work we had made, years ago. But, stung by disappointment, I just said, "They were so strong. They danced like crazy. They didn't care what anyone thought."

Jesse looked at me. "You had a hard time."

A sob escaped me, but I quelled the next one by tightening my throat. I sat down on the bed and felt the zipper of a coat under my thigh.

He pushed aside coats and hats and sat next to me. He smelled of beer and a pine-scented cologne I remembered from when he was seventeen. "I'm sorry. I should have been there for you. We were friends."

There were lines at his cheekbones, etched into his rubbery skin. I touched his hand, which was damp and swollen. His illness.

He took away his hand. "I should go."

I wiped a tear that had crept down my cheek. "But I haven't asked you anything. Like what have you been doing all these years?"

"Why do you want to know? You don't even like me."

"I do like you." I realized it was true. There was nothing left to forgive.

He got up and zipped up his coat.

"Can I see you again?" I asked. "You live around the corner."

I didn't think of asking him for his apartment number. I didn't think ahead, not to a few weeks later, when I would be standing in the vestibule of his building, staring at the mailboxes. Nor did I picture the moment five years later, when I would sit at my kitchen counter, read the paper, and find Jesse's obituary.

"Yeah." He walked out of my room and didn't look back. "I'm right here."

Restaurants with My Daughter

LAST WEEK, MY DAUGHTER Martha took me out for my birthday dinner. In the past her husband joined us, but this year Martha didn't bring him. I can't say I blame her — Devin can be cranky. Still, it would have been nice to be a family, all of us together for once.

Martha, like her father Abe, is always getting me to try new things in life. For my birthday, she wanted me to eat venison. I have never cared for venison. It has to do with *Bambi*, I think. I saw it with my mother when it was released again — was it the second or third time? My mother was glamorous, what you might call an aspiring socialite, but she always had time for me. She died very young, of a rare form of lung cancer, before I got to know her properly.

Martha kept saying, "Mum, venison is the specialty."

I tried to stall her, to appear open to her input. "Do you like venison?"

"It's an acquired taste, but I think you'll like it. Aren't you up for adventure?"

I reminded her that just last month she had refused my invitation to join me for the city's Summerlicious restaurant festival, the one where you get an expensive meal for a good price. She used work as an excuse. In her work habits, too, she is like her father. Abe worked all hours no matter how many times I told him that no one needed an insurance claim processed at midnight, no matter how desperate for the money.

I had ended up going alone to Scaramouche, a restaurant that has a good view of the city. It was there that I had the most delicious pea soup I've ever tasted. Velvety, aromatic, and not over-salted. It was vibrant green, like those pastures I saw in Niagara County the weekend Abe took me to a bed and breakfast for our anniversary.

Yet as delicious as the soup was, as I ate I couldn't help but picture someone shelling all the peas I imagined had gone into the soup. When the waiter came by to brush off my table — an undertaking I had never seen before — I pointed out the pea shelling to him. He nodded and smiled, his lips tight, as if he and I didn't know that it takes the better part of an hour to shell enough for one serving. I used to shell them each spring, when produce is at its best and when you don't pay five dollars for a carrot. Abe always wanted me to hire kitchen help, but I was not going to pay someone to do something I could do perfectly well on my own.

When I reminded Martha of the festival, and then added something about the pea soup so that maybe she'd experience regret and consider coming with me next time, she sighed. She tried again, pointing out that venison was leaner than beef, and didn't I want to make healthier food choices? But I wanted steak, had my heart set on it as soon as I knew we were coming to a French restaurant.

Martha had not intended to take me to a French restaurant in the first place. On the phone, she had asked whether I wanted Japanese or Thai. She and Devin eat all sorts of things, even sushi. Abe never understood this. He used to say, "Why would you pay good money to eat something raw?"

I told Martha that I didn't want either. I asked her if I could choose my own birthday dinner.

"Of course you can, Mum." Then she asked me if I wanted French food.

I have always been a Francophile. When I was nine, my mother came home wearing extravagant French stockings, and I couldn't stop touching her silky calves. That was before I realized that her ill-advised spending was killing my tailor father, slowly but surely.

"French would be lovely," I replied.

WHEN DINING AT A French restaurant, I usually choose steak. Once, I went with the veal and I regretted it. There is nothing better than a tender piece of steak, cooked medium rare, with a side of curled golden-and-purple shallots. I consider steak done properly to be a piece of heaven.

Martha's suggestion of venison had thrown me off. When the waiter came by to take our order, I stared at the menu, my eyes drawn to the description of the steak. *Bavette à l'échalote.* I studied French in school. Abe once told me I had a perfect accent.

Martha's fingers, including the one with the yellow diamond engagement ring, drummed on the table. As always, she had ordered without hesitation. Well, when you're earning six figures and are married to a corporate lawyer, you can afford to order quickly. You will always be able to choose something different the next time around.

"I can return, Madame," the waiter said.

He was tall for a Frenchman, very proper and a little bit of a snob. He reminded me of the waiter at Loire, that restaurant where Abe persuaded me to try caviar off his plate. Little bursts of salt on my tongue. I could smell the ocean. He offered to order me some but I refused — it was enough to have tasted his portion.

I looked up at Martha and my French waiter, and I told him that I would take the steak. "*La bavette.*"

"Ah, *Madame parle français.*"

"*J'ai étude...*"

"*Étudié,*" said Martha.

"*Étudié à l'école,*" I said.

"*Bravo,*" said the waiter.

Good service makes such a difference to one's dining experience.

Once he was gone I started to think about the possibility

that the steak would be served with herbed butter on it. Until recently, butter was my delight. I have always bought unsalted butter wholesale and frozen it, and brought out little pieces to place into a Versailles butter dish once belonging to my mother. "I hope they don't skimp on the butter," I said to Martha.

"Are you sure you should be having that?"

She was referring to my recent doctor's visit, during which Dr. Davis told me that I have elevated bad cholesterol. The good news was that my good cholesterol was up also. I had told Martha this, but as usual, she was dwelling on the negative.

In her negativity, she's very different from Abe. "Live a little, Hattie," he used to say to me. Abe always wanted to do more and take more risks, and he wanted me to join him. That attitude was shaped by the deprivation he suffered as a child of immigrants. He still ate like a Polish Jew, but he chose the most expensive food: the best pastrami cuts, the best sausage. Saturdays, at lunch, he ate bagels, cream cheese, and lox. Three bagels at a time. Abe used to take me to The Pickle Barrel once a month, and he ate there the way he did everything, with great gusto. I tried to caution him not to eat the fatty cuts of pastrami, but he didn't listen. I should have been firmer. Sometimes I think he would still be alive today if I had been more insistent about the pastrami. Then I remind myself that I am not to blame.

The night we celebrated our thirtieth anniversary in Paris, he presented me with a necklace of natural pearls. "Thirtieth is pearls, right?" I burst into tears. By that point we'd had breakfast at our four-star hotel, gone to see Monet at the Musée d'Orsay, had *macarons* at Ladurée, and eaten caviar at dinner. I was overwhelmed, bursting with happiness, but also overcome with guilt.

Part of my confusion was due to the fact that I had been wondering for some time what state our finances were in. I suspected that Abe was lying to me about his business, and the amount of debt he may have had, when he assured me that everything was fine. So I made him take back the pearls. I stood outside the jewelry store and watched him through the glass as he made the transaction. When he came out, his face was grey.

After Martha pointed out my error in ordering a dish with a lot of butter, I summoned the waiter again. Beside me, Martha smiled painfully.

On the menu was *Daurade aux amandes*, which I remembered was a type of fish, here made with almonds. I also remembered reading in *The Star* that fish is a heart-healthy food. It contains an oil called omega, which happens to be good for your skin as well as your heart. When the waiter returned, I asked him the name of the fish in English, and he said that it was sea bream.

"Ah yes," I said. Then I asked if there was butter in the fish.

He held the menu away from him as if he were farsighted. "*Alors, alors. Oui.* The almonds are made in butter sauce!"

"Oooh. But. Would you say the fish has as much butter as the steak?"

"Mum," said Martha.

"Martha, I'm asking a question." Young people are so reluctant about making inquiries. It was as if Martha were thirteen again and I was asking a clerk about an advertised discount!

"Well, *Madame*," the waiter said, "the chef puts extra butter on the steak. And with the fish, you could push the almond sauce a little to the side, *n'est-ce-pas?*"

"I could."

"And butter is good for you." He smiled, took the menu out of my hands, and disappeared into the kitchen.

"I guess I'm having fish," I said to Martha once the waiter was gone.

"Mum, he thought you'd decided."

"But he was in such a hurry."

Once he returned to serve other customers, I caught his eye again and motioned for him to approach. "I would like a glass of champagne, please."

Martha looked startled. "Really?"

"I have decided to indulge. It's my birthday, you see," I said to the waiter. "That is, if my daughter is okay with it. She's treating me."

"That's fine," Martha said. Her neck was red. I hadn't meant to offend her; simply I wanted to make sure she didn't over-extend herself. I had forgotten for a moment that she is no longer a cash-strapped student, but a well-paid career woman.

"And you, *Mademoiselle?*" The waiter winked at her and she smiled at him, and I must admit I felt a little left out, like when she and her dad used side against me. I wish for once she would take my side.

When the champagne arrived, it had miniature golden fireworks bursting up the flute. I drank half of it quickly, and it gave me a pleasant feeling on the way down. I don't have it often and I always forget its complexity: tangy, sharp, sweet.

While we waited for our food, I told Martha I was going to meet a friend for tea and Gauguin.

"I didn't know you were a fan."

"Oh yes! Those colours."

"They say he objectified Tahitian women."

"Oh, but he appreciated the female form. They're sexy, don't you think?"

"Mum!"

Young people never realize their mothers have interests beyond the scope of motherhood. I have always appreciated certain of life's appetites, and Abe always enjoyed my adventurousness in matters of the heart. I may have been frugal in life, but not in this particular department. He used to say, "Hattie, you surprise me." At least in this, I can say that I made him happy.

"Your dad always wanted me to drink champagne. But I wouldn't. It went straight to my head, you see!"

"I know."

"I didn't want to be like my mother. Did I tell you she overdrank? I think that's what killed her, in the end. They didn't say so, but I always thought so."

"I'm sure Dad understood."

"He never listened to me. He always asked me, 'Why do you see the worst in every situation?'"

Martha put her hand on my arm. "You did your best, Mum," she said, and I was ready to forgive her for flirting with the waiter, who in my opinion was not as patient with me as he should have been. Martha was just trying to make the dinner pleasant. When all is said and done, she's a good girl.

My sea bream was so tender that it flaked off in little bits under my fork. The almonds were blanched and drowned in butter. They were crunchy and sweet. At first, I pushed the sauce to the side as the waiter had advised. By the end of the meal, however, I had pulled the sauce back in toward the centre of the plate and mopped it up with pieces of baguette.

Martha had ordered the venison, and seemed to enjoy her meal. When she was done, she put her fork and knife at five o'clock on the plate, the way I had taught her when she was a child.

I sat back in my chair. "Maybe I shouldn't have eaten so much."

"Should I get the bill?"

"You're not ordering dessert?"

"If you want."

"Oh yes, I wouldn't mind."

When the waiter came, I said to him, "I think I'll indulge a little more."

"Pardon?"

Martha took over. "Could we see the dessert menu, please?"

"Of course."

The dessert menu was what I had expected, with all the traditional French pastries. There were *tartes*. I have a soft spot for *tarte aux abricots*. But I also like *crème brûlée*. The way the crust breaks under a fork to reveal the pale cream underneath.

When the waiter came back, Martha sent him away again.

"But I'm ready to order," I said.

"I didn't want him to wait too long, Mum."

"But that's his job!"

"I know, but it was taking a while."

"Fine."

"You always get mad about the smallest things!"

The waiter came back at that point, and I ordered the *crème brûlée*.

"Nothing for me, thanks," Martha said. "I'm sorry we're being so difficult."

"Not at all, *Mademoiselle*." He took away our dessert menus.

"Martha, that was very rude."

"What?"

"You didn't need to apologize."

"We have been fussy, don't you think?"

"No, I don't. He was doing his job."

"You think that because you pay someone you can treat them poorly."

"In life you have to ask for what you want. You don't have to make me look bad."

"You're right, Mom." She looked contrite and I was sorry about how things were going. I was going to tell her not to mind what I'd said, but she got up and went to the washroom.

While she was gone, the dessert came. I waited before I ate it, and when she came back, she said, "I'm not having dessert. Why did you wait?"

"Well." I was going to say something else but I changed my mind. It wasn't worth continuing this line of conversation. To make peace, I offered her some of my dessert. She took some with her coffee spoon.

"It's delicious."

"Yes, very well done."

"This is my favourite. I love the contrast between the crust and the cream."

I paused. "Why didn't you order some?"

She patted her stomach, which as far as I could see was flat as an ironing board. "I'm trying to be careful."

"Oh, don't be silly. You look beautiful."

She turned a bit red. "Thanks, Mum."

She wouldn't take any more of the *crème brûlée*, so I finished it alone.

While we waited for the cheque, I leaned over. "It's nice being us girls, right?"

She smiled.

"Are you and Devin taking a little break?"

"What? What the heck are you talking about?"

"Well, he's not here, so I assumed."

"Mum, he's just working."

"Oh, I see." Then I added, "Last year, I found him a touch disagreeable."

She looked even more irritated than before. "If you must

know, he was a little frustrated with you last year. So he opted out."

"He opted out?"

"Yes." Her face went through a few transformations. First it was frowning. Then her lips moved as if they wanted to add something. Then her eyes looked sad.

I looked down at my empty plate.

She apologized. "Okay," she said. "Occasionally Devin can be a little tense."

I wondered if she was going to add 'and so can you,' because sometimes I think about these things. But she didn't, bless her.

When the cheque came, she paid it.

"Not too much, I hope," I said.

"It's fine." She sounded annoyed again. She closed the cheque sleeve, rose, and took her purse. I had to scramble to pick mine up off the back of the chair and follow her. Our dinners always end like this, with us angry at each other. We argue about silly things and I always regret it. She is my daughter, after all, but I can never seem to get things right between us.

Outside, I invited her to join me for my art gallery outing scheduled for the next day.

"No thanks," she said, without looking up from her cellphone.

As we waited for the taxi that was going to take her back to her office, I thought again about the pearls Abe had offered me on our thirtieth wedding anniversary. I wish I had accepted them. I could have at least done that for him.

SALARY MAN

THE BLINDS BLINK OPEN like a sleepy eye. Shinjuku sky-scrapers shoot up from the ground, angular as combs. The light is bright, shatters into white stars whenever it hits a wall.

"Wow," Jeremy says to the empty room, and without think-ing, reaches for his phone.

That he's still angry at Lise only occurs to him once he hears the ringing. He realizes that he has no idea if she's at home or at work. The bedside clock reads eight, but is that a.m. or p.m. in Toronto? "Lise! I'm in the Hilton."

"Holy cow. How did you not know that beforehand?" From beyond comes a baby's wail. She must be in the pedi-atric department of their neighbourhood hospital, where she works as a registered nurse.

"Declan must be doing better than we thought." He carries

the cordless into the living space, surveying an off-white corner couch, a glass desk, and a single orchid in a slender vase.

"I was right to tell you to ask him for a raise," says Lise.

"You've never seen this many skyscrapers."

"Skyscrapers?"

"The architecture, the light. You would love it." Then, the question that has lingered for the past twenty hours, all the time he's been travelling. "Has Lowell been around?" he creaks out.

She doesn't seem to notice. "Why don't you call him?" Her voice fades as if she's moved her head away from the phone. "We're swamped."

"I wish you could see the view."

"Don't forget you're there to work," she says, zooming him right back into focus.

Like with making the phone call in the first place, he reacts automatically. "Give me a break, will you?"

"I'm just saying. Sometimes you get distracted."

FOR THE FIRST TWO thirds of the flight from Toronto to Tokyo, he'd brooded. He knew the fatigue magnified every image he held in his mind, but he couldn't help it. He needed to know what was what: how and when things started between Lise, his girlfriend of six years, and Lowell, his friend for twice as long. Had it been at their friend's engagement party, one year ago, during which Lowell and Lise had spent a lot of time together in the outdoor swimming pool? Or had it happened gradually, during the winter evenings when

Lowell came over to watch the hockey game, Saturday night after Saturday night, to the point where if he didn't show up, it seemed like a family member was missing?

Truth be told, he wasn't sure there was anything actually going on. But things felt serious enough to shake him.

What happened was this: four days before his flight, Jeremy had come home to find Lowell and Lise in front of their rented bungalow. Lowell was in the front yard, bent over, and seemed to be moving some flat stones. Sweat was at the base of his neck, below his newly buzzed hair. Nearby was a half-empty beer bottle. Lise sat on the first step of their house. She wore cut-offs, and her toenails were painted fluorescent orange.

Here's her husband, doing the heavy lifting, had been Jeremy's automatic thought. For a split second, before the anger set in, it was merely an observation without judgment.

"Declan let you off early, eh?" Lise's elbows were on her knees, her hands hanging, relaxed, between her slightly parted legs.

Jeremy's bowels felt like he'd eaten too many spicy wings the night before.

"Lowell is helping me set up my moss garden."

Her eyes widened, and Jeremy pictured two fluorescent green dragonflies, like the ones that caught them by surprise during their first walk together, years before, on Cherry Beach.

Lowell didn't say anything. Keeping his eyes lowered, he lifted a stone and grunted.

In the airplane, Jeremy's gut cramped so badly that he slumped down in his seat and squeezed his eyes shut until he finally fell asleep. He woke only when a stewardess pressed down gently on his right shoulder. Her hand was delicate.

That was the first hint of what was to come: everywhere he went in Japan, he would be treated with courtesy as fine as crepe paper.

When he checked into his hotel, the woman at the front desk warned him that his room wasn't ready. There was a couple there, she told him, pausing on each word as if it were a stone in a river that she was stepping on in an attempt not to fall.

"They don't want to leave?" he asked, still stupefied by emotional and physical fatigue.

"They are just married, so ..." She smiled, and he understood that she was trying to prod him out of himself, into the humour of a shared joke.

A small smile of his own made its way to the surface. "Right."

In the end, so he wouldn't have to wait, she gave him a different room. "It has a beautiful view," she said, and he nodded. By this point, he didn't care what the room looked like; he just wanted to lie down.

As soon as he got to the suite, he crossed to the bedroom and collapsed on the bed, face down, his still-shod feet dangling over the edge. He entered a darkness deep as a body bag.

Sometime in the night he was awakened by a woman screaming. Wails rose and fell over an orchestra soundtrack. He thought it strange that, in this luxury hotel, he could hear television from another room.

SINCE HIS MEETING ISN'T until lunch, he showers, dresses, and leaves his room. The elevator arrives in seconds, the doors gliding open with barely a rattle. A screen mounted above the doors shows, first, interior shots of the hotel, then a man and a woman dressing for a wedding. The man knots a black tie; someone zips up the woman's satin dress. They seem to be neither white nor Asian but a mix, presumably so that no viewer feels left out. The woman's bare shoulder flashes above her ivory neckline like a bronze doorknob. The couple enters a room before a crowd of onlookers, and walk up the aisle toward a podium. The next shot is of the man cupping the woman's chin.

Last year, Lowell told Jeremy he should marry Lise. Lowell was attending motivational seminars then, the kind where they gave him pithy idioms such as *Anything is Possible*, and vowed to help him find the *Roadmap to Success*. He had also started to work out and began internet dating. "They all want that," he said. "The ring, the house. My point is, don't wait too long."

But Lowell didn't know Lise, not really. Jeremy had overheard her tell her mom that she and Jeremy didn't want a public ceremony. They loved each other; they didn't need to show it.

Jeremy forces himself to take a breath, the way his G.P. recommended last year. That was after he landed in emergency with what he thought was heart trouble, but which was actually a panic attack. The G.P. had attributed it to overwork. Jeremy thought that it was likely caused by the past eight months of him acquiring too much responsibility, too quickly.

The G.P. also told him to quit smoking, something Lise had asked him to do for years. Jeremy has not heeded their advice. Smoking is his minor way of keeping part of himself out of the claws of the establishment, of remaining true to himself. Whatever that is. He isn't sure anymore, if he ever really knew. But now, on the heels of Lise's possible betrayal, his anger and pain wrestling, Jeremy's glad he didn't capitulate on the smoking. It's not going to kill him yet — he's relatively young, has a few years to go before he absolutely needs to quit.

In the lobby, the woman who checked him in is back behind the wrap-around reception counter. He doesn't remember her being so beautiful: her smooth forehead, the narrow bridge of her nose. Her black hair parted in the middle, swept back by an ivory comb into a thick bun. Her white blouse tucked into a navy pencil skirt. Over her left breast, a tag reads *Tomiko*.

This morning, he feels a courage that comes from rest. "I want to thank you."

"Pardon?"

"For the new room you gave me."

Her eyes flutter, she looks elsewhere, then returns her gaze to him. "I remember."

"The view, as you told me, is wonderful. You gave me a gift." He is thinking these exact words and is surprised that he's actually said them. He isn't usually so effusive.

"People often enjoy the top rooms, sir."

DECLAN HAD MENTIONED THE public baths.

Jeremy doesn't love getting naked in public, but since Tomiko assured him the bathing is strictly same-sex, he figures he can handle it. Besides, he doesn't feel ready to leave the hotel. What else should he do, apart from scarfing down the remaining green-tea chocolate snacks in his hotel room, which he ate before figuring out that they cost one hundred and fifteen yen — the equivalent of ten dollars each?

The baths are in the basement. Jeremy has to walk past the hotel's workout area to get there, and he averts his eyes from a row of men on the elliptical machines. These machines have always struck him as particularly boring and also existentially problematic, as they go nowhere. As for exercise: you train and become buff, for what? Only to spend the rest of your life maintaining all of that? A colossal waste of time.

Someone has left a copy of *The Economist* on a bench in the baths' locker room. It's open to an article on *karoshi*, described as a Japanese form of corporate suicide which translates to "death by overwork." The article describes a thirty-year-old man who died after putting in long hours of overtime at his automotive job. *I'm happiest when I can sleep*, he told his wife the week before he died.

Jeremy is startled by the clang of a locker being banged open. A man, naked but for a white towel around his waist, is pushing a knapsack into a locker. "Sorry."

The bathing room smells like iron and is filled with fog. There are two square pools, separated by a low tiled wall. On the side from which the steam rises sit two middle-aged men with closed eyes. Jeremy dawdles a bit, reluctant to drop his towel. He now has a gut, probably from what has become, over the years, a beer-a-day habit. He's also always been shy about his tallness. When he and Lise first made love, they saw afresh their height differential. Only after fits of giggles did they get the hang of it, how to match his long frame to her tiny one.

As he is about to step into a pool, someone says "No," and Jeremy almost slips.

One of the men, with a barrel chest and rubbery jowls, points to the wall, from which hang hand showers. They are all at waist level, so low to the ground that Jeremy assumed they were for children. The man gestures toward them, then to bottles hung on the wall, and says, "There are stools."

Jeremy upturns what he had mistaken for a bucket and sits down, knees splayed. He begins to wash, as the man's eyes bore into his back. His knees keep bumping his chin.

Afterward, it takes him a full minute to immerse himself in the searing bath water, but once in, he relaxes. The bath, the suite, Tomiko: he's never been this pampered. Is this what it's like to have money, then? The bath cocoons him and he closes his eyes.

DECLAN OWNS LINKAGE, A small but rapidly growing company that matches Toronto businesses with Asian manufacturers. He had started with Japan for sentimental reasons, having taught English in Japan after university.

Jeremy likes working for him — Lise was right about that.

He likes the work itself, would lose himself in each task. He feels the same way searching for products requested by the company as he does when doing a crossword: that same sharpness of focus and loss of time. Afterward, he would look at the clock in the corner of his screen and be surprised that an hour had passed.

Declan had asked Jeremy to do the Tokyo trip from his hospital bed. He stared at Jeremy, his balding forehead sweating and his skin yellow from a complication of the West Nile virus, caught while Declan camped on the Bruce Peninsula. It made Jeremy uncomfortable to see his normally fit boss look so weak.

"When were you supposed to leave?" Jeremy asked.

"I know it's rushed."

"It's just not the best time." He was thinking about how, only a few days before, he had come across Lowell gardening with Lise. He was still trying to decide what, if anything, to do about it.

"When Lise asked me to hire you, I wasn't sure it would work out," Declan said. "I think you've surprised yourself, right?"

LISE AND HER MOTHER talked about Jeremy's smarts frequently and usually in front of him. Claudette, Lise's mother, had once marvelled at how quickly he did both the Saturday Sudoku and the crossword. "What are you doing at that factory?" she'd asked, referring to his old job at a furniture warehouse.

"He just doesn't like to work hard," Lise said.

"She's right." Jeremy blushed, then smiled because Lise knew him so well.

His own mother, too, had once declared that his brain would get him places. And it had. He had been the first in his family to go to university. After that, though, he saw no need to use it further, at least not in the realm of work. Beyond a fundamental discomfort about becoming one of the masses — a discomfort he shared with Lowell — he didn't see the point in becoming a successful career man. He wanted a low-key life: hanging with Lise, going to the occasional hockey game with Lowell. He wanted just enough money to get by.

Lise was the first person to demand more from him. It was Lise who asked him to leave his job as a stock manager at the warehouse. And when he moved to Declan's company, it was Lise who talked to him about getting a raise.

At first, he thought she only wanted him to tap into his unused potential. But then he began to notice that she seemed to want more and more things. At first glance, what she asked for did not seem frivolous. She didn't yearn for clothes, jewelry, or makeup. Instead she talked about new paint, furniture, and potting soil. In their life together, in which things were often up in the air, what she coveted seemed to signify a longing for permanence.

Jeremy wonders when Lise had started to imagine him as a member of the rat race. When did the girl who liked going to the Scarborough Bluffs to sit on a rock and watch the sunset, become the girl who hankered for so much stuff?

He wondered if she had been like this all along. Had he fallen in love with one person, only to discover over time that she is someone else? Only now, it's too late. He doesn't want to leave.

STILL IN THE BATH, Jeremy's eyes open. He's had two thoughts. One: that the things Lise wants are those that bring her beauty. Two: that the old pattern they fell into on the phone this morning — her trying to re-focus him, him fighting her efforts — is a good sign. It means she's still got a stake in him.

He starts to wonder if, for Lise, there's a choice involved. If how he conducts himself on this trip will impact how things turn out between them.

DECLAN HAD ADVISED JEREMY that the Japanese were big on convention. "Bow, don't shake hands. And — you know me, I have to say the obvious — be on time."

The Tokyo company, Sujimichi, makes handmade fabric upholstery, which an upscale Toronto furniture store has requested. Jeremy's job is to establish a relationship with the owners, Ren Watanabe and his father, Akeno. He's good at this kind of initial contact; he's got a knack for small talk. "You're great with the plebs," Declan jokes.

Jeremy gets to the hotel restaurant early, so he's already seated when Ren arrives. Ren has the dense and bouncy physique of a jogger. Like every Japanese businessman Jeremy has seen pass through the lobby, he wears a black suit, white shirt, and black brogues. His father is ill, Ren tells him, and will have to meet Jeremy tomorrow, during their scheduled factory tour. He has arranged for a driver to pick Jeremy up in the morning.

"Online business would have been better. But my father is old-fashioned." Ren hands Declan's contract back to Jeremy. "If you don't mind, we will sign it tomorrow, with my father."

So Declan was right in suggesting that Watanabe senior wanted to put a face to Linkage. Ren leans forward. "Would you like a beer?" The beer is stronger than Jeremy is used to, and he feels a buzz more quickly than expected. Ren has already finished half of his when he asks, "You have visited the Tokyo Imperial Palace?"

"Not yet."

"The palace reflects the history of Japan."

"I was thinking of starting by buying a present for my girlfriend."

"That's very important, indeed. Do you know where to purchase it?"

"Kiddyland?"

"The toy store?"

Tomiko had recommended it. "I was told that adults enjoy it too."

"Of course."

An hour later, they've enumerated Toronto tourist sites, they've compared Japanese and Canadian climates, and Ren has invited Jeremy to dinner. "Food is a very important part of Japanese culture," Ren says. Then, he adds, "You should visit the Harajuku girls." He explains that these are young women who dress up like dolls. He grins. "They just wanna have fun."

"Pardon?"

"A little joke, Mr. Evans. Please excuse me."

Only then does he recognize the Cyndi Lauper reference. Jeremy's shoulders relax, and he smiles at Ren.

HUNDREDS OF MEN AND women traverse at the Shinjuku crossing, which Declan told him is the busiest intersection in the world. Most are businessmen. They walk fast, their brief-cases close to their hips. Jeremy and Lowell used to mock these kinds of people, men they considered bland, with no aspirations beyond work. These men seem to Jeremy to be the living dead.

Jeremy has a moment of doubt when he glances down at his own suit, which he hadn't bothered to change out of after his meeting with Ren. What happened to the guy who used to loaf about, reading Kurt Vonnegut? What happened to the person Lise met at an open mic night, when they were both newly minted university students, just arrived in the big city?

Kiddyland takes up five floors and is filled with tchotchkes that Lise would call useless: flowered phone cases, plush animals, tiny plastic replicas of sushi. Jeremy, who has a row of McDonald's snack-pack toys on the rim of his office computer screen, blinks away tears from a sudden happiness. He's the proverbial kid in the candy store, spins around a few times before starting to touch objects, to pick them up and examine them.

Lise sometimes surprises him. Last year, at a Kitchener craft fair, she paused at a table of artisanal glass swans, so Jeremy bought some for her. When they got home, she lined them up on her dresser: male, female, and goslings. Remembering this, Jeremy finds the perfect present for Lise: tiny glass creatures, which he guesses are Japanese anime characters. He chooses only one, for they are exorbitantly expensive. Though he's counting on the success of the meeting with Ren, and on that raise he's sure to ask for now, he doesn't want to push his luck. For himself, he picks out a pair of chopsticks shaped like Star Wars lightsabers.

On an upstairs floor is a waist-high circular platform with two robots that remind him of the Transformers he used to play with as a kid. Each robot, one blue and one red, has a wire attached to it that leads to a square box with a lever.

Beside him is a pudgy boy with red cheeks, who looks about ten. "You play?"

"Definitely! How?"

The boy grabs hold of one of the levers, and the blue robot comes to life. With a grinding of gears, it marches toward the red robot and kicks it. The red robot skids to the edge of the platform. "Do you see?"

Jeremy grabs the red robot's lever. For the next few minutes their robots wrestle. First one robot falls, then the other. Jeremy experiences the thrill he used to get when he and Lowell played video games back in university. That adrenalin rush, the sheer joy of it, the seamlessness between his intent to move a character and its onscreen actions. Every time he and Lowell played, there was a competitiveness, the kind he tried to hide, but was betrayed by his quickening breath. Eventually, he would shake Lowell's hand, but that initial feeling lingered, a feeling that bordered on hatred.

A shard of pain catches at the base of Jeremy's throat. He should have known it would lead nowhere good when he made those changes to his life. When he thinks about it, that was when Lowell betrayed him: when he became the type of guy they had always despised.

The kid's robot spins off the table.

"Not bad for a guy who's out of practice, eh?" Jeremy feels patches of sweat in his armpits, hidden by his jacket.

The boy crouches to retrieve his robot from under a shelf of toy bullet trains.

"Another round?" Jeremy asks.

"No, thank you." The boy gives him a slight bow.

"Aw, come on."

JEREMY STARES AT HIMSELF in the mirror as he dresses for dinner with Ren. He's wearing his second suit; there's no getting around it, he'll have to wear the first one again for tomorrow's meeting with Mr. Watanabe.

Both suits have been tailored to his long limbs, and the cut of the jacket gives him a bit of bulk, especially around his shoulders. He straightens up, rather than slouching as he is wont to do. He's not a bad-looking man, come to think of it. That sharp chin, the evenly set blue eyes. In his bespoke suit, he looks like he could be very competent. Which is what he is of course — otherwise, would Declan have given him this job?

He is a man who has been sent here to do a job, a man staying in a suite with floor-to-ceiling windows and a panoramic view. He will land this account, persuade Declan to give him a raise, and give Lise what she wants. He will present himself to her as a man with resources. He will fight for her.

THE RESTAURANT REN TAKES him to seats about ten people. A Japanese couple is already eating when Jeremy and Ren enter. The woman has perfect posture and wears an ankle-length skirt. She looks around, assesses Jeremy, and turns back to her companion. The room is hushed save for the clinking of dishes and the syncopated hissing of things plunging in fat. There is a circular counter, behind which a chef cooks.

"Best tempura in town." Ren pulls a chair out for Jeremy.

The first dish to arrive appears to be small, cut vegetables — Japanese pickles, Ren explains. The jewelled pieces glisten: royal purple, forest green, lemon yellow. Then the hot dishes: mushrooms curled like tiny fists; beans like green, wrinkled sea animals; rectangular slices of peach-coloured eggplant. "You see," Ren says, "in Japan, presentation and taste are equally important."

Thirsty after sitting in traffic for an hour, Jeremy gulps at the carafe of sake that Ren has ordered. The sake warms as it hits his stomach. He focuses on his chopsticks, bites into a sour pickle. "You know what I love about Japan? It's how thought-out things are. Like those low walls along the subway platforms, in front of the tracks. Making everyone line up. Ingenious."

After a few seconds, Ren's eyes clear. "Ah! No, Mr. Evans. Those are for another purpose. For the Japanese businessman, there is so much pressure, you see. Those barriers that you speak of, they are to prevent people from jumping." Ren picks up his drink and swallows a few times. "More and more suicides, every year." He leans forward and speaks almost conspiratorially. "The government cannot do anything about it. In Japan, it is a very respectable thing, to kill one's self. You have heard about *kamikaze* pilots. There is also the practice of *seppuku*, which is honorable suicide."

"It seems a little extreme," says Jeremy.

"Ah, no," Ren says. "It was very respectable, for those in the war."

"I mean in business," Jeremy says.

"You don't know what is happening. Some companies, they have two books. One for the government, with fake work hours, and one for real hours. Most people, they work many hours of overtime, but they do not record them."

Jeremy wants to ask whether this is the case in Ren's factory, whether his father, too, has two sets of books. But for once, Jeremy's good sense gets the better of him, and he stops himself from posing the question just as it starts to form. He thinks to himself Lise would approve of his self-control, since it has to do with keeping his job. He tips more sake into his mouth.

The tempura arrives. There are fish bones (which Ren

assures him are a delicacy), prawn heads, and potato-like vegetables. He bites into an eggy, salty piece of heart-shaped fish — "Kissing Fish," Ren tells him — dipped in a sauce, not soy, though possibly fermented. He drinks more sake, for the sweet alcohol complements the salty, juicy food so well. He's never tasted anything so delicious. He closes his eyes, and when he opens them, Ren is smiling at him.

"You know, Mr. Evans, the generations are different. My father, he works for work's sake. But for myself, this is why I work so hard. Eating like this. Living like this. Do you agree?"

"Yes. Yes, I do agree." He finds, to his surprise, that he believes it.

Behind the counter, the chef dips morsels into a vat of oil, and lifts them out again with a giant slotted spoon. He affects a concentration that borders on religious fervour. Each time he hands over a dish, he studies their faces, as if to ensure that they're enjoying it.

The waitress treads in soundless slippers, anticipating their needs before they themselves are aware of them. When she brings more food, she rearranges the other dishes so that they are equidistant. Jeremy feels an expansive happiness: toward the chef, the waitress, Ren. Toward Lise. He thinks briefly of Lowell and feels a pulse of pity for him, who has never experienced a meal like this. The pity is almost instantly replaced by anger, like a slammed shutter.

But Lise. On the way home in a taxi, Jeremy decides he will phone her. He wants to give her something, anything. He wants to tell her that he's starting to understand what she wants. *The food, the service*, he'll say to her. *It was art. I get it. This is what money can buy. It can make you part of someone's dream, part of something greater than yourself.*

He wants to grow old with her. In his mind's eye he sees them on a patio swing at twilight, drinking beers. Crickets chirping, the smell of cut grass. He'll cup the hot, dry heel of one of her feet, calloused from all those hours she stands during her nursing shifts.

From the open windows of his cab, he watches fluorescent signs blink. Hordes of people walk by, their feet clip-clopping on the sidewalk. Their conversations roar. He can't believe this many people are out this late — it must be one in the morning.

By the time he gets back to the hotel, the alcohol-induced euphoria has started to seep away. The bed, with its cloud-white sheets and fluffed-up pillows, awaits. Nevertheless, he dials, first Lise's work, then home. At home, the phone rings on and on, in a tinny kind of way. Outside the enormous windows, a fog has risen, obscuring the skyscrapers' blinking lights.

JEREMY DREAMS THAT HE and Lise are at the Scarborough Bluffs. Their jeans rolled up to their knees, they taunt the water, seeing how far they can walk in without getting their clothes wet. Lise squints her eyes at him. Above them, gulls screech.

He wakes to a woman's screams, coming from the room above. Wails rise and fall, followed by the low tones of someone who sounds angry. Someone male. Jeremy's heart speeds up. He's not hearing someone's television, he realizes. Someone is harassing a woman. His eyes fly open. He listens a bit longer, and as he listens, he grows indignant. How dare someone interfere with the delicacy of his experience, especially with something as sordid as, what, abuse? His imagination forms a variety of scenarios, all involving a woman who looks like Tomiko, being bullied by a large, faceless man. Now he wavers between anger and fear.

Somewhere, from a long-drawn-out domestic argument that lies in his past, he hears Lise's frustrated voice: *I want you to move! Up, down. I don't care which way.*

The reception desk answers his call immediately. "Tomiko?" He listens to silence. "I'm sorry, I thought you were someone else." He gives the woman on the line his room number and explains what he's heard. "I'm sure things are fine."

"I will check." At first uncertain, the female voice is now amused.

"Because you never know."

"Thank you, sir."

It takes him a full hour to fall asleep, what with his rising headache and dry throat, both signifying tomorrow's hangover. Finally, he gets up, swallows a sleeping pill, and sleeps.

THE PHONE WAKES HIM. The blinds are open and from his bed he can see the blinking light of a single airplane across the night sky.

"Mr. Evans? It's Tomiko."

"Yes?" He feels as if someone is dredging him up from a lake.

"I wanted to say thank you. For alerting us to a problem."

He rubs the sleep out of his eyes.

"You called, before, about a noise?"

"Right. Is everything okay?"

"I wanted to say thank you."

Well, alright, she doesn't want to tell him. She's a professional, after all.

"It has been taken care of," she says.

He is suffused with a rare contentment. Once she has hung up, he turns his head into the pillow, which smells of orchids, and smiles.

Sometime later, he wakes up for a second time. The light-grey sky outside his window tells him it's morning. Then he looks at the clock.

It's nine-oh-eight.

Crap. He's supposed to be downstairs, meeting Ren and Mr. Watanabe to visit the factory.

Jumping out of bed, he retches, but manages to keep whatever is left of last night's meal down. Ren's card is in his wallet, but where is his wallet? He finds it in the back pocket of his pants, at the foot of his bed. Without thinking, he dials his cell phone, which will cost a fortune in long-distance rates. "Ren? I'm sorry. I'll be down in five minutes."

"Fine." Ren's voice seems to come from far away.

Wishing he had time to take a shower — if only to rinse off his skin, which emanates a scent of oil and fermentation

— he washes his face and brushes his teeth. It takes him another two minutes to dress. The clock now reads nine thirteen.

In the elevator, the wedding video is playing, looping as Jeremy makes his way down to the lobby. The bride and groom hold hands, then separate as the movie begins again.

The lobby's cacophony, of unknown languages, of children and women and men, hits him when the elevator doors open. Halfway across the room, Ren is standing in front of one of the lobby's revolving doors, holding the elbow of an old man. The man, who looks like an older version of Ren, seems to be wriggling out of Ren's grasp. Ren finally cedes and looks around him: first over his shoulder, toward the interior of the lobby; then down at his wrist where, even from where he stands, Jeremy can see the flash of a watch; then out the revolving door into the street, and finally over his shoulder again. It's as if he's trying to decide something.

In the Afternoon

THE LAST TIME I saw all of them together, we were standing in their beige marbled vestibule: Jackie, clouded in Givenchy, and Richard, in a charcoal suit, bending to kiss baby Suzette, who sat in the crook of my arm as if it were a rocking chair.

I wanted them to go. It was always the same: my regret that Richard was leaving, and my eagerness at becoming the mistress of his house.

Richard turned to me. "I want to show you something."

"Richard," said Jackie.

"*Un petit moment.* Come, Catherine."

Jackie looked at me and rolled her eyes, as though to confirm that we both knew how Richard could be. Back then I liked her pretty well, though I disdained her a bit, too. I felt she didn't have much control over her husband. It was only later that I realized, where Richard was concerned, she had always been more powerful than me.

I gave Suzette to her mother and she protested, but then turned placid. She was an easy baby, which I appreciated only a few years ago, once I had my own kids. Then I followed Richard up the stairs.

Richard was tall and had a kind of middle-aged professorial handsomeness. He had a lick of untamed hair on the top front of his head, and he wore wire-rimmed glasses and expensive suits. He was a diplomat who'd landed in diplomacy by accident because his father had been in it. He didn't like his work, but he was good at it. He had an attitude of respect for his elders in the job, a stance that bordered on subservience, but didn't quite make it there. He was a political man too, and he could, when required, become rapidly dissembling.

We went into the spare bedroom, which was cluttered with the things the family no longer used. It was where Richard kept his stash of videotapes. These were stacked haphazardly, on bookshelves, on dressers, and on the floor. Some of the boxes were open, with cassettes peeking out like turtles emerging from their shells.

On a stand, the VCR radiated heat from having been on for some time. Richard reached for a remote.

"Look," he said. He showed me a clip. "It's a documentary about Artaud. The playwright."

Onscreen, the actor who played Artaud sat at a table with a man and a woman. Artaud ate soup while the woman watched.

"That's the poet Prevel and his wife," whispered Richard.

As I watched, Artaud and the woman held a philosophical discussion about the nature of good and evil. Prevel's attention drifted; he scribbled in a notebook. Twice Artaud interrupted his discourse to comment on the soup. "What is in this?" he asked the woman. "It has a velvety texture." The woman smiled.

Richard turned to me. "You see. Even during a philosophical discussion, Artaud appreciates the here and now, the sensations he is experiencing at that moment. In this scene, unlike Prevel, Artaud eats. He wants to savour every particle of that soup."

He ejected the cassette and handed it to me. "Here."

"Are you sure?" I asked. I wouldn't be able to watch it at home. My mother would wander into our living room and wonder why I wasn't upstairs, studying. My father would frown on it, too. He had a mixed attitude toward Western culture, and liked only Japanese film.

In fact, it was due to Japanese cinema that I was in Richard's house; it was what had brought Richard and my father together. At the time, my father was engineering plans for the construction of a library at the French consulate. Richard expressed his longing to include a film section, and my father mentioned Kurosawa's *Ran* in order to argue that the Japanese could take a Western story and make it better. After a while, the two talked about their children — and that was when Richard asked if I had babysitting experience.

I took the tape. I liked having something of Richard's, and

would add it to other things of his, kept in a box under my desk. My mother was a good housekeeper, but she never touched my study space.

"Richard!" Jackie called from downstairs.

Like her husband, Jackie was tall. She came from a wealthy expatriate Moroccan family living in New York. Short for "Jacqueline," "Jackie" was coined by Richard during a phase of his of loving all things American. He and Jackie met at a charity ball in Manhattan. Jackie finished her degree in art history at Vassar and moved to Toronto with Richard.

She had put the baby down on the floor. "Dadada," said Suzette, shaking her mother's keys.

"Nice shoes," I said to Jackie. She had Mary Jane shoes on: beige, with white semicircles along each side. The colour matched her coat, against which her dark hair lay in a solid mass.

"A Mother's Day present. Do you believe Richard picked them out himself?" She was glowing, as always when she was about to go out. She was like a horse kept too much in the stable, chomping at the bit.

Richard smiled. "We'd better go."

"Oh God, I haven't told you anything, have I?" Jackie went through a list of what Suzette should eat. "There's an egg on the stove."

"Only the whites," said Richard. "She doesn't like the yolk."

FOR MONTHS I'D BEEN exploring their house slowly: first admiring, then touching. The last few weeks, I'd become braver, picking things up, smelling stuff, reading books. I could feel myself ready to try something more. Perhaps, for the first time, I would go up to their bedroom. Jackie had a closet full of clothes, which I wanted to try on. The couple was leaving for the rest of the day, and I would have time to look around.

Suzette cooed. She had begun crying when Jackie took back her keys, so I'd picked her up, and she stopped fussing. Since the day I'd met her, she trusted me. I was good with kids, but I speculated that there were also other forces at work. I'd been told by white acquaintances that I never seemed to *feel* anything, that my face looked expressionless. This seemed to me to be a common misconception about Asians, and I wondered whether Suzette had a kind of racial blindness when it came to me, and didn't recognize that I did, in fact, have strong feelings and that they must have registered on my face, to be perceived by people who knew me well.

Suzette was as beautiful as the Victorian house her parents rented. How could she not be? She had gorgeous parents, who doted on her in the way of parents destined to have only one child. Her father dressed her in handmade clothes. Almost every time I went to their house, a new outfit that Richard had bought — a dress or knitted cap or wool coat — was lying on the entrance table.

Now she was wearing what looked like an antique cotton gown, with hand-crocheted lace edging the sleeves. The dress was too flimsy for the winter day, and I thought of putting her in a sweater, but I didn't. Part of me thought it would be a punishment for Jackie, if her kid caught a cold. I guess I did resent her a bit. But then I felt guilty, and I hugged Suzette to give her warmth.

Looking back, I shudder to think of how callous I was with the baby. When my kids were young I considered each babysitter carefully, trying to peer through each young girl's professionalism to see if there was anything menacing underneath. But really, what can you tell from someone's face?

IN THE KITCHEN, I sat Suzette in her high chair and gave her the whites of two hard-boiled eggs and, for dessert, raspberries that I found in the fridge. She picked up each raspberry as if she were holding a jewel. "Hmmm," she gurgled.

"Hmmm."

While she ate, I rummaged through the fridge. There were the remains of a chocolate mousse cake; I took off a jigsaw piece that no one would miss. In the door was a bottle of carrot juice. Fresh juices are supposed to detoxify the body, so I poured out a glass and drank it.

When I turned around, the baby had stained her dress. The bib I'd put on was totally impractical, a handmade woven piece given to Jackie by her mother, and raspberry juice had leaked around it. I wiped it, but a little was left behind, like a rose blossom.

Suzette batted her spoon and looked at me.

"Do you want to walk around the house?" I asked. We often played a game where we moved from room to room. Whenever one of us got bored, we moved on. This activity had a double purpose, for it both entertained her and gave me more chances to browse through the house and absorb its possessions. Once, while playing the game, I found a smooth, green bronze sculpture of a man. I touched it with the tip of my tongue.

My parents are Buddhists, though since coming to Canada they've practised nothing. But back then I was tantalized by the religion, albeit the Western kind. In my mind, the kind of Buddhism my friends were infatuated with had nothing to do with what my parents had left behind, and I saw the Western version — which I learned from reading Whitman — as a way of helping me cope with the boredom of my studies, of life in general. My school friends gave me books which for the most part I skimmed. The result was that I didn't have a very thorough understanding of the subject. I thought that being Buddhist meant that I was supposed to appreciate not just everything around me in totality, but also every object's uniqueness: the thingness of a thing. What I didn't know until several years later, after I attended a public lecture on Zen Buddhism, is that I was also supposed to be able to let go of stuff.

In front of the living room fireplace was a low glass table. Suzette started taking rocks out of a ceramic bowl on a side table and bringing them over to the glass table, where she lined them up in a row. She took one at a time, which was all she could manage because she was crawling. I was admiring how evenly apart she was placing the rocks, when she bumped her head on the edge of the table and started yelling.

I picked her up. "Let me see."

A blue egg rose on her forehead. *What on earth would I tell Richard?* I thought.

Richard loved that baby. It was Richard who changed her because apparently Jackie hated bodily fluids and tended to throw up when faced with bowel movements. It was Richard who put her to bed. And it was Richard who had showed a flustered Jackie and me how to give Suzette a bottle, after reading how from a magazine. Jackie had responded tensely to Richard's advice. "I read too," she'd said to me in front of Richard, and I detected a low buzz of hysteria in her tone. "But those articles bore me so much after a while!"

What on earth would I tell Richard? After an afternoon with me, Suzette was a mess. Egg was in her hair, and her dress was ruined, and now her forehead was bruised.

I picked her up. "Bath time."

Suzette shimmered like a miniature Buddha in the bath. She slapped her hands on the water and laughed when I gave an exaggerated cry.

Once, her head slipped below the water. I have to admit that I didn't take her out right away. By then she had become, to me, like all the other things in the house: just something to be admired. They didn't always feel real. For a moment, I watched her. Her eyes were like pebbles at the bottom of a lake. On her head, soft tendrils of hair waved to and fro.

Eventually, I picked her up and wrapped her in a towel. She tried to take a breath, which gurgled in her throat. When I saw that she was about to yell, I gave her pecks of kisses all over her face, which stopped her scream in its tracks.

AFTER I STOPPED BABYSITTING for Richard and Jackie, I no longer watched films. Once, my husband took me to Éric Rohmer's *L'Amour l'après-midi*, and afterward my face was wet. He said, "Well, this wasn't supposed to make you unhappy."

Back when I knew Richard, watching movies was like reading issues of *Vanity Fair*, copies of which I kept under physics books in my bedroom closet, only to be taken out when my father was out of the house so I could admire the artfully placed necklines and hems, the sheerness of the silks. Reading magazines, watching movies: these were both a waste of time, and in our family, flitting away time was taboo. We counted hours by the work to be done in them.

Like Richard, I was groomed to be one thing. My parents always expected me to be a doctor. I was a natural at chemistry, biology, physics, and I would eventually go to medical school. But, again like Richard, I always looked for the gaps in the path I was supposed to take.

There is the machinery of living. Then there is everything outside life, everything involving pleasure.

AFTER THE BATH, BEDTIME. As usual, Suzette said nothing as I placed her on her stomach. She put her head to the side and kept her eyes open.

The walls of her room were painted yellow, the light filtering through the cotton curtains the yellowish-grey of a late winter's afternoon. On the wall was a single poster of some marionettes, with *15 Novembre 1990* and some other Italian words at the top. The mobile over the baby's crib was a replica of a merry-go-round, with the horses spinning lazily to the tune of Brahms's *Lullaby*. Suzette turned on her back and watched, her eyes blinking as she followed the horses twirling round and round.

Downstairs, the phone rang. I backed up quietly, then ran down to the entranceway and answered on the fourth ring.

"How is everything?" Richard asked.

"Fine. She has a bit of a bruise. Bumped her head on the glass table."

"I've told Jackie we have to get a bumper pad."

"A bumper pad?"

"You wrap it around the table like piping."

"Ah." To belie the nervousness in my voice, because really, his daughter had nearly drowned, I said, "She loves bedtime!"

I heard nothing.

"The mobile," I said. "The music."

"Very much," he agreed.

"Richard —"

"Yes?"

What else did I want to tell him? That the carousel above Suzette's bed was amazing? That, along with the yellow walls and the light, it made the room and Suzette look charmed? That his whole life was fantastic? Perhaps he knew that already. For although he clearly wanted to pursue a career in film, he had never done so. He knew his family counted on him. He was responsible for his house and everything in it.

"The food here is something," Richard said. "I'm bringing you cake."

AFTER PEEKING IN ON Suzette, who was sleeping, I went up to the third floor, where Jackie and Richard retreated when things below got hectic. A master bedroom and an ensuite bathroom had been installed in what had been the hundred-year-old house's attic. The bathroom was gorgeous. Heated tiles and an antique dresser gave it a blend of contemporary cool and ancient warmth. Above a clawed bathtub, a narrow glass shelf displayed perfume bottles and soap figurines of young boys playing lutes.

I turned on the tap and poured in some lavender bubble bath. Even before the tub was full, I undressed and slipped into the water. I put foot mask cream on my feet. The lavender water lapping at my knees and my fingers rubbing my feet in small circles made it seem as if someone else were touching me.

I stepped out of the bath and drained it, using a washcloth that was hanging on the edge of the tub to wipe off the ring of suds. I wrapped a towel under my armpits. For a moment I stood, and lavender steamed off my feet. For once, no one was trying to get into a bathroom I was in. No younger sister yelling and trying to fiddle with the lock.

On the back of the toilet seat, a cosmetic bag was wide open, as if Jackie had been in too much of a hurry to close it properly. A mascara stick had fallen out onto the floor; I picked it up and applied it. The black leaked onto my eyelids.

Buried in the bag was a pair of rusty eyebrow tweezers. I brought them to my face in front of the mirror and considered. Superimposed on my olive forehead, tanned from the summer sun, the tweezers looked like a tiny spear. I plucked my eyebrows until a bare patch appeared between them. A few strands of hair were left on the tweezers, but I left them there and put the tweezers back where I found them.

On a dresser in the bedroom were three photos. One was black-and-white, of a middle-aged lady in a pillbox hat who looked like Jackie. A second was a close-up of Suzette as a newborn, cocooned in a striped hospital blanket. The last was a silver-framed photograph of Richard holding the baby. In the photo Suzette was about four months old, wearing a white crocheted blanket, the folds of which looked like an angel's drooping wings. Richard's earlobes emerged like water drops from under a navy knitted hat. In the background was a grainy Ferris wheel, as if the photo were taken not only from a distance, but also in the rain.

I opened Jackie's closet. Her clothes were few, but expensive. I tried on one of her dresses: a wool-cotton blend printed with large crimson roses. The dress was too big for my frame, which was more boyish than curvy. Still, I felt regal and pictured myself as Richard's wife, at one of the monthly receptions that they threw for visiting diplomats. Like Jackie, I would mill about. I would stop at each group of guests and chat about the latest political scandal. I would smile to ugly and good-looking men alike.

THE WEEK BEFORE, I thought he was getting ready to leave her.

I'd arrived when they were preparing for one of their parties. I was always hired for these events. Even though people would often mistake me for the kitchen help, I enjoyed being there, participating in the elegance of these evenings.

As I was hanging my coat up in the hall closet, I heard their voices from the pantry off the kitchen.

"Where are the sugary treats?" asked Richard.

"There are none," said Jackie. "Just savoury."

"What?" The plates he put down on the serving table clattered. Then he looked up and saw me. "Hello, Catherine."

I wonder if it was around this time that Jackie started feeling disappointed. She had everything she wanted, and it was a glamorous life. But perhaps the political conversations bored her. Perhaps the men were polite, but distant, their wives bitter and resenting their younger female counterparts, the spouses who fit the image of the political wife more cleanly than they did. Jackie was young, but maybe she was starting to see that she would eventually become them, and she didn't like it. I saw her looking in the mirror once, and, even though I couldn't see a single line on her face, she said, "Crow's feet."

These days, like her, I search for signs of aging, astonished that the mirror shows nothing, that others won't see the decline I know is happening.

Afterwards, Richard took me up to the spare room.

"The guests are coming any minute," said Jackie.

Richard nodded and ushered me up anyways. I looked apologetically at Jackie as I went, hoping to soften the blow of her husband's carelessness.

Instead of turning on the VCR, he handed me a cassette.

"I want you to see this," he said. "*L'Amour l'après-midi*. In English, it's *Love in the Afternoon*. Rohmer." He kept his hand on the cassette. "It's about a lawyer who suffers from boredom. The afternoons are hard for him. So each day, he meets a lover." He paused. "After lunch is the hardest time."

"Why doesn't he go home to his wife?" I asked.

He looked at me as if, for the first time, he saw who he was talking to. I was seventeen years old, with pink-tinged hair that I had coloured in a moment of rebellion. I had flawless skin. I was not good looking, but I was young. I was a clean slate.

"Because she is part of the bourgeoisie of course," he said, half mockingly.

I thought for a moment. "Why don't you make movies, like you want to?"

"Oh no." He turned away and started sorting the tapes. I saw that I had been right: he couldn't give up his life as it was, the life he loved.

IN THE MASTER BEDROOM, there was a queen-sized bed pushed up to the wall. The sheets were embossed with Jackie's initials. I took off Jackie's dress and slipped between the sheets. After a minute, I put my hands under, too.

It was as I was touching myself that Richard walked in. Once he saw me, he looked away, and then at the floor, at the nest of his wife's dress.

He stared out the window, from which you could see one of the maples, its branches bare save for a few patches of snow. "Please," he said. "Get up."

If I got up I would be naked in front of him, so I stayed where I was.

He backed up. "Jackie's still at the party. She was having fun." His voice was half pleading. I'd like to think that he was offering me an apology.

THE NEXT WEEK, I went to their house as usual.

Jackie opened the door and stared at me. She had a steeliness that I hadn't seen before. Where before she may have been intimidated by me, now she definitely was not.

"Hello, Catherine."

I wondered why she wasn't opening the door further to welcome me in, and tried to see beyond her, inside the house. Richard was nowhere in sight, though he must have been home.

I smiled and waited for her to let me in.

"I have bad news," she said. "The office has cut our budget."

I nodded. I still thought she was going to let me in.

"We can't pay you anymore."

I stared. She waited. I heard Suzette's babbling from the house.

"Suzette has a cold," she explained. "I wouldn't want you to get sick."

"What about Saturday?" I asked.

"We really can't afford you," she said. But then she blinked, and a tear appeared on one of her lashes. "I'm sorry," she said. "I won't forget Suzette's first babysitter."

FOR SIX MONTHS, I was furious at Richard. And even after the anger disappeared, I was left with an aching under my ribs. The soreness was located in the place where Suzette's stomach used to press against mine. I missed Suzette. Mostly, I missed holding her. I had not realized until then that I loved her.

Years after I'd stopped thinking of them, my father called. Richard had left his wife, he said, and Jackie was accusing Richard of abusing their child. In order to obtain part custody of the child, Richard needed a letter from me. Ideally, I would testify that I had never seen Richard act inappropriately toward Suzette. "I don't think Richard will win," said my father, "but your opinion will be respected."

By then I was no longer preoccupied with the thingness of things. I had abandoned this interest and instead embraced the chaos of daily life. I was in love with my first child. When she was born, I told myself that I would kill anyone who might wish to harm her.

So I wrote the letter. I thought to myself, what can you really know about someone? But I didn't think he was guilty.

I wrote that, after his outings with Jackie, Richard mounted the stairs two by two to check on his daughter. That although Richard didn't cook, he cleaned up. That I saw him, spotted with diamonds of refracted light coming through the window, holding Suzette and whispering, to her, passages from *L'Amour l'après-midi*.

LUCK

WHEN NOREEN COMPLIMENTS ALISON on her cake, Alison smiles a tiny, hardwood canoe of a smile at odds with her pudgy, optimistic face, a face that used to look on the world as if it were one long drink of water. I recognize this smile from the days before I had Archana, back when people told me that losing my pregnancies was for the best.

"It's from a mix," says Alison.

"Still," adds Sophie, the only blonde one here and the most level-headed.

We're comforting Alison because although the rest of our kids have been moving around for a while, Alison's son Malcolm can't even turn over by himself yet. We've been trying to tone down talk of our babies' milestones, but despite our best efforts and innate Canadian politeness, the subject of our babies' progress keeps resurfacing.

The five of us meet every two weeks at one another's houses, to talk about baby problems, brag about our kids, and alleviate the boredom of being new parents. Today, we're spread out on an Ikea carpet and navy-blue, plush armchairs. A cherry-wood coffee table, which has been pushed against the wall, displays a single plastic sippy cup and some primary-coloured bibs. Cups of coffee are lined up on the chimney mantelpiece. Toys are scattered on the floor. We call one of these toys — a transparent plastic bowl with a long handle — the popcorn maker. When it's pushed, small marbles fly up inside the dome in a burst of blossoming "fireworks."

There are of course the babies. Most of them are fat, and many of them are crawling. Soft, disoriented quadrupeds, they bump into furniture and, turning, redirect themselves toward another bright thing that has caught their attention.

We dig into the cake. It's spongy and iced — normally something I would hate, but after my daughter's arrival, I revel in everything sensuous, regardless of where it comes from. Having children has awakened my senses: I experience life in an exaggerated way. I constantly feel pushed over the edge, sharpened to a point, nearly tipping into crisis.

Noreen, who's been sitting on her hands, studies the icing cresting over the cake. "Still trying to shed pounds, ladies."

"I made it with Splenda," says Alison.

"Really?"

Sophie smiles as she helps herself to a second piece.

"Nothing is fat-free." She jogged here and is wearing sky-blue spandex pants and white Nike shoes.

"Maybe a little." Noreen cuts off a triangle, which crumbles as she lifts it. "Oops."

AT THE ADOPTION AGENCY in Addis Ababa, the Ethiopian adoption agent kept smiling as she said, "There has been a delay."

Despite having been warned of this very thing, we were annoyed.

"How much time?" Peter's a man to get straight to the point.

"One week?"

"One week?"

"One week." This time the woman spoke more firmly.

Peter's considerable shoulders tensed. He's built like a footballer, but he's the most gentle person I know. Except when he has to wait for something. And we'd waited three years.

"Please," said the agent. "You will have time for sights. You know Ethiopia?"

I put my hand on Peter's arm. "We expected this. Let's figure out what we can do."

We walked back to the hotel through black-paved streets. Pink garbage bags rose in the breeze like flamingoes. From behind a fence towered an AIDS-prevention poster. At every corner, small children tried to sell us tissue packages. They touched our legs and bargained. We'd been told that men recruited the children to run this business. Of course, there were worse things than selling tissue. We bought a pack from each group.

At the hotel, we lay on our backs on our single beds. The heat exhausted me. I pictured the street toddlers scampering at our feet, their meant-to-be-pleasing faces running with sweat. Their attitudes were their only weapons. When I looked closely, I thought I could see in their eyes the fear of not making their quota. A waiter at the hotel restaurant with whom we'd become friends had informed us that street children who didn't sell enough tissue were beaten.

I debated taking a shower in the trickle of water the hotel offered.

Peter opened the guide book. "How about the Simien Mountains?"

"Are we fit enough?"

"How hard do you think it is?" It was true that back home we did a lot of walking.

"I can't stop thinking about —"

"Which is exactly why we have to."

"WHO'S GOING BACK TO work?" asks Noreen. She's the least attractive among us, but she doesn't care. She wears heavy dark-framed glasses and rarely brushes her thick black hair. We don't blame her for neglecting herself, though, because her son's a handful. He crawls so fast we call him "The Commando."

"I am." I want to shout this from the rooftops. I can't wait!

Guiltily, I baptize my daughter with my hand. Her scalp is moss on a warm stone.

"Yeah," says Sophie. "I like my job."

"I didn't want to," says Noreen, "but John got mad. He said, 'You will go back to work after one year, you will build a career.'"

"That's extreme."

"Can you discuss it?" Marjorie is a grade school teacher. The minute Emily was born, Marjorie was already thinking about her next child.

"He's not a discusser."

"Men." Sophie works in human resources. She's good at managing humans.

"What about you, Marjorie?" asks Noreen.

"We're going to try to make a go at it with one salary. Childhood goes by so fast."

"Lucky," says Noreen.

TRAVELLERS HAVE ALWAYS EXTOLLED the beauty of the Simien Mountains in northern Ethiopia. From a distance, they were ragged, giant peaks. Up close, they're pock-marked rocks with pockets of bleached grasses and delicate white flowers. But it's the light that was the most amazing. Just before dusk, the dying sun streaked the stones with pastel pinks, yellows, and blues, as if a schoolchild had run along the ranges and painted them with swathes of primary-coloured chalk.

Although it was hard going, I kept walking. If you get tired on a hike, you're supposed to work through it. I thought about our future child. Like most Amharic Ethiopians, he would be dark and high-cheeked boned. He would be delicate. I felt sure that although he would feel out of place in Canada at first, we could figure things out.

At noon on the first day, we sheltered under tall boulders to eat bread and peanut butter, which we had bought for a fortune in Addis before boarding the plane to Gondar, a small town southwest of the mountains.

Peter folded a piece of bread over a gob of peanut butter. "What are you thinking?"

"You know. I just want to make sure we're not stealing anyone's baby."

"It's that whole Madonna thing. It freaked you out." A few months before our papers had gone through, Madonna adopted an orphan boy from Malawi. A journalist discovered that, in fact, the boy had a father. "We checked and rechecked the agency."

"But is it really better? I mean, than helping the locals help themselves?"

"Liz, we've talked about this."

WE'RE ALL STILL EATING. I love food and don't feel guilty: I'm skinny no matter what I eat.

Sophie helps herself to another cracker with cream cheese. "I'm still breastfeeding, so."

At this, Noreen asks, "I wonder what Lisa is doing?"

Lisa was one of our earlier group members, a school teacher obviously used to supervising a classroom. After getting to know her, I'd begun to think that her controlling nature must have caused her to leave situations often. She was the only one of us who couldn't breastfeed. Either her milk wasn't coming in fast enough, or she didn't have enough milk — I forget the exact nature of the trouble. It bothered her, though. She knew that we all thought, but didn't say, that *breast is best*.

Most of us breastfeed — at this very moment, some of us sit on the floor, leaning against the couch, cradling a cushion in an elbow; one of us is on the custom-made glider; others are on the couch itself, wrapping breastfeeding pillows around our waists like buoys.

Lisa had to give her baby, Zachariah, the bottle. When she fed him, she refused to look at us. Zachariah drank with great gulps that could be heard, even with all the slurping and sucking going on.

BY THE SECOND DAY of trekking, I felt like I had the flu. My knapsack seemed heavy, despite the fact that it contained only water and a camera; a mule carried the rest of our gear. I put one foot carefully in front of the other and watched the red sand form a tide line around my ankles.

In the late afternoon, we stopped on a flat green plain to set up our tents. From there, we could see the green peaks of other mountains and the serpentine brown paths winding through them.

A tiny shepherd's hut stood in the middle of the plain. In the distance, goats bleated. At one point, a small boy brought a baby goat to entertain us. The goat stumbled, and the boy, smiling, admonished it and lifted up its hind legs so that it wobbled toward us. Peter gave the boy a birr, and he left us.

That night, we cooked a lentil stew. As we waited for the stew to be ready, we sprawled on stones around the fire, taking occasional breaks to go outside and breathe some smoke-free air. A rag hung over the door to the hut, and every time someone went in or out, frigid mountain air was let in.

At one point, the mule leader opened the curtain and hesitated on the threshold, wondering if he could join us for dinner. We normally invited everyone, including our guide, our armed guard, and the mule keeper, to eat with us, and we also paid for all the groceries. Since many families in this area rarely had enough to feed their families, this arrangement made sense.

"Okay!" I hissed to Peter. "Let him come in or go out. But let him decide, already."

Peter, who was seated on a boulder, teetered slightly. "What's wrong with you?"

By the third day of trekking, I could barely put on my knapsack after rest stops. Our guide suggested that I ride one of the mules. I could only just hold onto the mule's mane. Each time the path steepened, the man leading my mule smiled back at me in reassurance.

I wanted to go home. I wanted my bed, my bathroom, my new wood-floored semi-detached house — the one we had bought in preparation for the child.

"Let's turn around," I told Peter that evening.

"Do you know how few westerners get to come here?"

The landscape was spectacular, but I didn't care. "I need to go back."

THE LAST TIME LISA came, she packed up her baby's stuff carefully, like someone doing a puzzle. I caught up to her in Noreen's foyer. "Are you okay?"

"Yeah."

"It really doesn't matter how you feed the baby. There's so much more to it than that."

Lisa slotted a bottle into the side of her diaper bag. "I read that it's not about the breast itself, but about the physical bond. You can get it from giving the baby a bottle."

"Exactly!"

After she finished placing Zachariah in the front carrier, she began putting on her jacket. The days were getting colder. We often debated about whether it was good to have our babies in the fall — you're so sedentary the first few weeks anyway — or whether it would have been better to give birth in the spring, when the longer days keep you from sinking into postpartum depression.

"So we'll see you next week?"

"Yeah."

For weeks after that, although Lisa never showed up, I kept her on our group email list.

WHEN WE GOT BACK to Addis, a test confirmed what I already knew: I was pregnant.

"Oh my God," I said out loud to myself in the empty bath-room. I came out and told Peter.

Peter's eyes widened. "How is that possible?"

"It must be the hormones from the adoption process."

"Awesome, right?" Now that he was over the astonishment, Peter's face was full of joy.

"I read that morning sickness means the pregnancy is a good one." Suddenly I felt confident that things would turn out differently — this time around.

"Well, we're about to have a whole lot of work on our hands."

At the time, I misunderstood him. I thought he was talking only about what was inside me, the baby he and I had made.

"OH, GRACE," SAYS SOPHIE. Grace has pulled herself up and knocked over a lamp.

Like her mother, Grace has a sunny, open disposition. She smiles frequently, sprouting a dimple on her left cheek. When Sophie told us she had rolled over for the first time, we thought it was a fluke.

"Could it have been a one-time thing?" I'd asked Sophie then.

"That's what I thought, but then she did it again. Here." Sophie put Grace on a sky-blue blanket covered with yellow ducks. Grace lifted one leg up and over, as if she were doing a yoga stretch, and flipped over onto her stomach. Then, before her toe had barely grazed a duck, she rolled again onto her back.

"I thought you were kidding!" The merriment in Noreen's voice sounded genuine.

WHEN WE TOLD THE agency woman that we'd decided not to adopt, she smiled. But her eyes were calculating: she was already planning where else to place the child. Without looking at her, I signed the release papers.

"You'll regret it," said Peter quietly.

"It doesn't seem right, now."

"But why? We could have two. We have the means."

Even after our all-night discussion in our hotel room, he continued to pursue this line of argument, and I continued to push back. I didn't know then that the disappointment behind his eyes would last through my pregnancy.

"It doesn't make sense."

When we returned home, my mother, too, asked me why I'd changed my mind. She's a church-going woman. Although she had grieved our decision to adopt, she had reconciled herself to it quickly, especially because adoption gelled with her religious beliefs.

"What about the other child?" she asked.

My belly was already softening. I patted it possessively. "It was meant to be."

How could I tell either Peter or my mother that I felt as if I had won the lottery? That I had personally succeeded where others before me had failed?

I TURN TOWARD THE other mothers in our group. "Archana's finally cruising!"

We named our daughter after Peter's Indian grandmother. It's a funny name for her because she doesn't look a bit like her father's side. She's as pale as I am, freckled, and her hair is slightly red, like the just-ripening part of a peach. Peter jokes that he's got some questions for the mailman. He doesn't give a damn though. I see Peter and Arch together, how he blows on her belly to make her giggle like mad.

All the other babies in our group, apart from Malcolm and Arch, have been pulling themselves along the floor for a few weeks, and I'd started fretting out loud to the other moms.

Now, watching Archana inch forward on Alison's carpet, Sophie says, "See? Nothing to worry about."

Noreen looks up. "Those developmental milestones are off, anyway."

We try not to stare at Malcolm, who's not yet able to sit up. He's looking right back at us. Alison has propped him up with pillows. He's like the emperor with no clothes.

In the kitchen, I help Alison clean up. "Great spread."

"Malcolm's so quiet that I can get anything done." She's doing the dishes with her back to me. "Liz, what am I going to do?"

Although I know she can't see me, I nod.

"The doctor's sending us for tests next week."

"I'm sure it's all very preliminary."

I can't help thinking of a recurring dream I've been having recently. In the dream, the OB nurse hands me Archana, over and over again, and each time I'm amazed at how beautiful she looks — not in an objective way, I can already see she's going to have my own Greco-Roman nose — but in that human kind of way, with ten wiggling toes and a neck that

works, and on this neck, an active, thinking head, like a miniature, solid hard hat.

Alison stands with her fingers under the water, too long
to be testing its temperature. As I stack the last plate and
turn to go back into the living room, she speaks, her voice
so low I almost don't hear her through the running water.
"Don't tell the others, okay?"

AS I BECAME HEAVIER, I began comparing myself to other
pregnant women. I had stopped eating raw cheeses and fish and
would criticize women who did. I would look at women on
the street and ask Peter, "How many pounds do you think?
Do you think she's thinking of gestational diabetes at all?"

One night, we had dinner with our neighbours Linda
and George, who were also expecting. Linda talked about
the genetic tests they were doing, and about how they were
arranging for cord blood banking. If their child fell ill, they
would be able to use his own genetic material to help him.

"I wouldn't mind —" I started saying.

Peter interrupted me. "That setup's a little too pessimistic
for my taste."

George took a large bite of chicken stew. "I told her it was
another corporation playing on the population's fears around
pregnancy. She wouldn't listen."

"Hey." Linda punched her husband lightly on the arm.

"Just kidding." He swallowed. "We think of it as another
type of insurance."

Later, I brought popcorn to the TV room, where Peter and

George were watching football. A commercial for the latest SUV — vehicles Peter hated — was on.

They started talking about people we knew, those who did not yet have children, and those who had become pregnant in the last few years. "What happens to these girls when they get pregnant?" George was asking.

"I know," Peter said. "They get so competitive."

"Like it's a game," George said. "Who can have the better pregnancy? Who can still look good? And look out if a girl is doing something like smoking. Then they want to kill them. They're constantly at each other's throats."

Peter added: "Like gladiators whose audience is chanting for blood."

IN ALISON'S LIVING ROOM, we're splayed out like starfish on rocks. Around us, our babies use the furniture to pull themselves up. Only Malcolm is still seated in his tugboat of cushions, as if he will suddenly be carried off to a more understanding place.

But then, Sophie says, "Look, guys."

Like an old man who's finally found his cane, Malcolm grasps the couch fully with his left hand and pulls himself to a standing position. Holding onto the couch with one hand, he sways, roly-poly, and makes contented guttural noises.

"Malcolm, yay!"

"Oh, my God." Alison dashes toward him and then keeps her hands outstretched in space, as if she is afraid that touching him will upset his balance.

Malcolm drops. Alison grabs him and lifts him up in the air in front of her, then kisses him on both cheeks. "Baby!" She shakes her head in disbelief, already transitioning from feeling self-pity to mocking herself. "Ladies, I was so worried."

Later, at her kitchen table, Alison slumps over on her forearms. "I didn't know what to do."

I touch her shoulder. "It was never your fault."

ONE IN THREE WOMEN have miscarriages. About them, I have little to add. The blood, the cramps, the shame. Was it that beer, the one I had before I knew I was pregnant? Finally, the forgetting: you find yourself still mentally ticking off baby names, until you remember.

After the second miscarriage, I joined an online support group. I entered my grief idly onto the screen and felt immediately better. Once, an anonymous user typed: *Did you drink coffee during your pregnancy? That could have done it.*

THAT EVENING, WHILE ARCHANA sleeps, Peter and I talk in our living room.

"It's all about luck, isn't it?" I say to him. "The whole pregnancy thing. The babies."

"I never thought otherwise."

"And Malcolm walking. Just good fortune."

Peter taps his fingers on our coffee table. "There's a problem with your thesis. It eliminates the need for action."

Just outside the corners of his mouth are small grey-green

shadows of disappointment. They've been there since I told him I no longer wanted to adopt.

He asks, "Did Alison take Malcolm for therapy?"

"I don't know."

"She should have."

IN THE STREETS OF Addis Ababa, children gathered around us. They butted against our legs like moths, chanting the name of the tissue brand they were selling: "Softies, softies." Their thick-lashed eyes widened at the prospect of our wallets opening. And perhaps each one of them was thinking — viciously, competitively, or maybe only warily and willing himself not to care — that, among the others shuffling their wares, he alone would be chosen.

INHERITANCE

WHAT IS THAT INSTINCTIVE terror gripping Josie when a shape makes its way toward her, parting the water in which she swims? A slim, oblong body; a short head with a blunt snout; an unhappy-looking mouth. The grey fish with a white belly undulates toward her in the way particular to its kind, and Josie knows it for what it is.

"Leo!"

She spins in circles, her legs egg-beating. She was enjoying the snorkelling, a surprising fact given that she usually feels uneasy in natural settings. The water had been cool, and the explosion of colourful fish schooling below the surface had startled her out of her initial unease.

Now she's seen the shark, though, and her heart accelerates.

"Interesting, the way they're attracted to a motor's sound,"

Leo says from behind her. "They came because of the boat."

Josie whirls around. "You scared me!"

His eyes are hard to make out behind his snorkel mask. "I was under."

"I didn't expect sharks," she says. The boat is far away, its white sail bobbing like a buoy, peeking now and then above the mild grey surf. Her voice wavers. "This guy looks hungry."

"It's instinctive," says Leo as he treads water beside her. "Something in you knows it's a natural predator. This is one of the gentler species, though. A whitetip. Only three attacks on the international shark file."

"There's a file? Well, that's comforting."

He ignores her sarcasm. "If you consider the number of people swimming in oceans, even off this peninsula alone, the number of shark attacks is statistically negligible. Let's assume there are one hundred people a day in this area. Last year there was one shark attack. So you have a one percent chance of being attacked."

Unlike Josie, Leo is not breathing hard. Already an excellent swimmer, he became an even better one last summer, which he spent in Nova Scotia working in a marine biology lab. He's about to start graduate school so he knows what he's talking about. Because of that, and his scientist's approach to the world — devoid of irrational fears — Josie would normally have total confidence in him. But a sensation that he's not telling the entire truth itches her. Since they boarded the boat after lunch, he's been keeping his distance.

The Leo Josie knows is a person infused with contentment.

Once, as they were walking home from campus, he said, seemingly apropos of nothing, "Isn't life amazing?" And it is, for him. He's happily on his way to a career he loves, he has a girlfriend, and — for the moment at least — they have no petty cash-flow problems.

Leo doesn't seem to have a temper, either. Once, she'd kissed another guy. It had happened at a house party, at the home of a friend of a friend. The guy had kissed Josie in the corridor of the overloud party. His kiss was wet, over-vigorous as it always is with good-looking men, who are too egotistical to consult women about the quality of their embrace. That night, she joked with Leo about the guy's over-productive salivary glands. It was so early on in their relationship — she and Leo had not yet moved in together, and she was only spending weekends in his low-rise apartment — that she made nothing of it. Leo's reaction, in the days following, was the only time she'd seen him angry — and even then, his was such a discreet resentment that she could have been imagining it.

LEO IS THE SON of German immigrants. His father is a retired engineer living in Elmira, Ontario, and his mother is the stay-at-home variety, and a church volunteer. His father is a dour man, probably because of the war, during which he lost six of his eight siblings. Leo thinks his own cheerful streak is inherited from his mother's side. He considers his happiness a dike in the face of the slow trickle of his father's grimness.

Leo has come to see Josie as an integral part of his life — a well-deserved one. Since meeting her, he hasn't for a second considered seeing anyone else. Why go elsewhere when you've already found what you want? He pictures life without Josie and feels empty.

He looks at her now, in the water. Her medium-length light-brown hair is slicked back off her face and she still looks beautiful. That square jaw and just slightly too-wide face. Those hazel eyes. He pulls down his mask, so he can see her properly, and grins. "Isn't this wonderful?"

Josie watches his reddish beard, which has grown to an impressive length, dip into the waves. His blue eyes squint. A clean smell of fish hangs in the air. From high in the blue sky come the squeaky laughs of gulls. Josie's and Leo's heads are close. Josie is glad that she came. Maybe there is time to regroup, after all.

JOSIE IS THE TYPE of person who moves toward stability even as she retreats from it. Her father, an unpublished writer, spent twenty summer vacations writing the same novel. Whenever he was writing, everybody knew it — they would try to talk to him, and he wouldn't actually hear anything they said. It wasn't as if he were deaf, it was more as if he were in a sepia-coloured photograph of a writer at work.

As a little girl, Josie didn't mind his self-absorption, but as she grew older she became aware of the damage it caused. Her parents argued. Her mother, who as a medical secretary was the breadwinner, urged her husband to finish his book or abandon it — advice he found hurtful. Her mother died of breast cancer when Josie was fifteen. Josie believed that her father's decades of spinning his tale and getting nowhere was possibly to blame for her mother's stress, which had surely exacerbated her illness.

Though Josie tells herself she will never be like either of them, she knows there is part of her that is like her father — an aspect that obsessively explores possibilities. Josie is frightened of letting this part take over. One reason she fell in love with Leo is the fact that he never wavers from his goals. Another is that he succeeds in everything he sets out to do.

Sometimes, she likes to ask him about his work. But she doesn't like to experience it. Insects and humidity were not what she pictured when Leo suggested that they take a holiday in a tropical setting.

Yesterday they took a walk through a mangrove forest. Leo talked her into it by telling her they would be walking on planks set up for the purpose; she wouldn't need to get too close to the wet ground. The forest, which was really a swamp because that is where mangroves grow, was mottled green and grey, so thick were the mangrove branches. Mosquitos buzzed and bit. Sweat bathed their foreheads.

After they had been walking for some minutes, Josie noticed large spiders in the trees. She looked up and shivered. "Ugh."

"Look at that." Leo went off the planks, his hiking boots squelching in the muck. "Why do you think their legs are so long?"

"The better to scare us with?"

He looked at her. "Oh, sorry. Let's get going."

For a moment, she thought he'd lingered on purpose. He knew she hated anything that crawled.

A few years before, the day after the unwanted kissing incident, Josie had baked a cake in Leo's kitchen. Since she was leaving for the library, she had asked him to cover the cooled cake, which was a golden upside down pineapple masterpiece. Covering food was a precaution they both took because the apartment building was infested with cockroaches. The following morning, she came into the kitchen and saw a thumb-long red bug hanging on the golden fringe, its antenna waving as if with pleasure as it nibbled.

"Leo!"

He came into the kitchen, rubbing his hair with a towel. "Oops."

"Disgusting."

He got closer. "Do you know that cockroaches will outlive us for millennia after we're dead?"

"Can you help me get rid of it, please?"

But he was already backing out. "I've got a class."

Back then, she'd wondered if he'd relished her disgust. She wonders this again.

EVERY ONCE IN A while, Leo experiences a deep fury at various happenings — and also at people, especially when they disappoint him. He's surprised by this powerful emotion, and, in the few hours it takes for his anger to ebb away completely, takes time to examine it. Last summer, when a fellow student made a calculation mistake during the course of one of their spatio-temporal analyzes of green crab, Leo was so furious that he imagined himself grabbing the student by the shoulders and shaking him vigorously. He left the room to settle himself before speaking to him, and noticed that the student seemed afraid. When, later that night, he considered the incident, he thought to himself that it was his innate perfectionism that had caused him to lose his temper over such a small mistake — after all, their supervisor would have caught it later that week. He thought about how scared the student had been, and concluded that he was someone who had been coddled and was unused to criticism, and so had reacted strongly to Leo's angry tone.

He speculates that it is not his own anger that he's feeling but, rather, his father's. Leo once read in a newspaper that researchers in the field of epigenetics may have found evidence of what trauma survivors have suspected for years, which is that emotions can be inherited, passed down from one generation to the next. Leo knew that his father had suffered war trauma, and perhaps his feelings — his despair and anger at the conscription and subsequent death of his six brothers — had slithered their way into Leo's genes, like a seemingly benign snake that turned out to be poisonous. Leo is satisfied with this hypothesis. If the emotion isn't his, he can learn to control it. He can observe the phenomenon, as he does marine life, take note of it, attempt to analyze the conditions under which it arises, and strive to eliminate them.

The trouble is that it's so hard to become a detached observer. When Josie was careless in the past, it set off a slew of feelings in Leo, from grief to fury to anguish. But her unpredictability is what draws him to her. She startles him with her questions about identity and lifestyle. She's smart. She asks him about his work in a way that shows him that over the five years they've been together, through his under-graduate career and into his graduate studies, she's actually listened to him and understands his work.

Lately, his anger has reappeared. Leo has begun to notice Josie's increased awareness of other men. Other women, too — something he first saw with a kind of startle, before realizing that, of course, it makes sense, it's in keeping with her open-minded character. When he sees her attention wandering, Leo practises withdrawing from the anger that assaults him. The ire arranges itself into the shape of a man, a double of Leo. Leo observes this second self with a scien-tist's dispassion. He is curious about what this second Leo might do.

Bobbing in the deep ocean on a brilliant afternoon, Leo instead focuses his attention on one of the great moments of what is, overall, a satisfying existence. Leo #1, as he has come to know the part of himself that withdraws from anger, believes that this trip will refocus his girlfriend's attention to him.

He points his chin toward the water. "There are lionfish down there. Shall we?"

Josie adjusts her mask over the freckled landscape of

her cheeks, and her hair catches in the elastic band. "Ouch."

Leo #2, the double, is filled with a kind of satisfaction for her small moment of discomfort. His grin expands as if to take in everything around them. From about a hundred metres away, the captain of their chartered boat yells out that they're halfway through their time in the water.

"What's he like, the tour operator?" Josie asks. Having spent the boat trip lounging on the coiled ropes in the boat's stern, she hadn't met the guy.

"A fisherman glad for the extra cash, I think. Shall we?"

Josie shivers as if she's reluctant to dunk her head in the water again. "Let's," she says, before placing the tube into her mouth.

JOSIE AND LEO'S ISLAND is off most tourists' maps. No one over the age of thirty comes here. Large hotels have not yet made an appearance. There is only one hostel, run by an expatriate German woman. She's a single mother who had a child with one of the locals, a ten-year-old boy who has his mother's dirty-blonde hair. The walls of the hostel are painted in pastel colours: blue, pink, and yellow. Iguanas are everywhere, their throats pulsing lime-green whenever someone approaches them to take a closer look.

The place is set up for loungers. There are paperbacks and rickety wooden tables. Old editions of *Lonely Planet* and *The Rough Guide* gather sand and dust on bookshelves next to seashells and sand dollars. There are dirty ashtrays, some half-filled with butts even at ten in the morning. Men and women in bathing suits hang out in this room. The men are usually shirtless and sunburnt. The women wear cut-off denim shorts over their suits.

The weather is almost always perfect, save for warm afternoon showers. Many of the hostellers spend their days going back and forth between the sandfly-ridden, narrow beaches that border the mangrove swamps. Many have been bitten by mosquitos because the tourists can't be bothered to use repellent. The guests stay here as long as possible. Divers linger until the onset of hurricane season. Young people about to go home decide instead to take a gap year. Others choose to quit their jobs back home and settle on the island until their savings run out.

Leo would never, even for a second, consider staying forever on an island like this — unless there were an oceanic lab. He's too curious, too in love with the life of the mind, to sit and merely exist. Josie understands this is precisely why she's with him.

Once, Josie decided to try living the lifestyle encouraged by the hostel's environment. She's seen others spend hours in the outdoor-style living room, with only some cigarettes and an old moldy copy of *The Road* to sustain them. But Josie couldn't do it. She sat in one of the sagging couches and read Pablo Neruda and, after an hour, she found herself drifting and irritable — not remembering a word of the book, itching to jump up and do something.

Josie appreciates being relaxed, but she also feels uneasy and needs to shake things up. Which is what she did yesterday.

As Leo was having a nap, Josie went downstairs to the open-air eating area for a snack. She was eating crackers and peanut butter when a woman her age came down the stairs and made her way to the communal hotplate. She wore cut-offs and an emerald bikini, and had freckled skin and small breasts. Her red hair was pulled back into a high ponytail, and she had green eyes and eyebrows so pale they disappeared. Josie saw that she wore no makeup.

The woman joined Josie at her table and set a plate of scrambled eggs in front of her. After some chewing and swallowing, she said, "You were here with your boyfriend yesterday, right?"

"Probably."

"You're not thinking of making this place your home?" She arched her eyebrows in such a way that conveyed to Josie she was being sarcastic.

The day before, Josie and Leo had been discussing their plans for the fall. While Leo works on his graduate degree, Josie would study to become a teacher. Josie is enough of a grown-up to understand that money is important. Becoming a teacher will allow her to make enough to live on without sacrificing too much time studying. It would also free up her summers to do other things. Travel, for instance. Or to get to know other men and women. She still holds single life in the back of her mind, even while she suspects that Leo might have a very different view of things.

"I'm like you," said the woman. "I have plans." She pushed the rest of the scrambled eggs onto a fork with a crust of bread, then tossed the whole thing into her mouth as she rose to sit on a large stained cotton couch. "You're not in a rush, are you?" She patted the seat beside her in an invitation.

"Who is?" Josie sat.

Her name was Marina, and she had a scholarship to the Emily Carr School of Art in Vancouver. She talked about her girlfriend, with whom she was going to live, though she had been with both sexes. "I've always said, I date people."

As Marina spoke, Josie felt unable to say a word. There was a stone lodged in her chest. She became aware of the filaments of her nose hairs waving in and out as she breathed.

Marina put her legs on Josie's lap, and that spot burned. Marina said, "You're not like the others here, escaping real life. You're solid. You know what you want. I like that."

Josie felt an actual pain in her chest.

"What's wrong?"

"I just wonder if it's the right thing."

"What do you mean?"

"Keeping a straight path in life without considering anything outside of it. It's kind of selling out, isn't it?"

"I didn't mean to say that I don't want to veer off the path a little," said Marina. Then she leaned over to kiss Josie.

Marina's lips tasted like strawberry lip gloss. Her skin was dry and smelled of sea salt.

Josie thought she heard something and half-turned, but it was just some palm fronds blown across the tiled floor.

The rest of the day went on as it always did, with showers,

then snapper fish tacos at their favourite food shack. When she spoke to Leo in the evening, he seemed the same as usual.

UNDERWATER, JOSIE WATCHES A lionfish with its stunning red, black, and white fireworks of spines, a show that belies its poisonous nature. Perhaps one eighth of her mind — and here she realizes how much Leo's sense of the world in numbers has influenced her — is distracted. As she surfaces, she dreams of yesterday's tacos as she treads water, waiting for Leo to emerge from the water. The fish in the tacos was so fresh that it lacked any kind of fishy smell; she almost didn't recognize it as fish. And the avocados! Like butter!

The sunlight is dwindling and Leo is still nowhere to be found. She marvels at his breath-holding abilities. Josie plunges her head back into the water.

The sharks slither past, come close and leave, as if they have been thinking of engaging her, but keep changing their minds. In the fading light, she can no longer see the white on their fins. Something startles them, for they spin around all at once and swim away.

When she emerges and spits out the breathing tube, she locates the thing that has triggered them; the captain has turned on the engine to alert the snorkellers that it's almost time to leave. She frowns. Has it already been an hour? Could she have lost track of time to such an extent? But then she realizes, from the swell of the waves, that the wind is picking up, and decides that they're being called back early due to approaching inclement weather. A few metres away, Leo is already swimming toward the boat, obviously expecting her to follow.

She starts to go after him, her eyes trained on his head and on the tour boat in front of him, which through the waves alternates between disappearing and reappearing. Life jackets that are darkening in the fading light jut out from its trapezoidal roof.

She puts her head down into the water for a moment and notices that the whitetips are back, swimming under her, swerving, almost touching the top of her legs. When she looks up again, she sees Leo climb up the boat's ladder and swing his right leg over the gunwale.

She's fifty metres away from the boat when it begins to move. "Hey!" she shouts, and swallows some salt water. She tries to swim faster, but she's tired and it's getting harder to propel herself forward in the roughening waves.

After a minute or two she gets closer and realizes that the boat has stopped. Thank goodness. She sees the heads of people, just peeking over the railings.

Then, the motor's roar returns, and the boat starts moving again.

Josie treads water in sheer disbelief. Her heart speeds up, her limbs stiff from her recent efforts. When she feels something rough brush against her thigh, her bladder seizes, warming the water around her middle. A breaker lulls, and she sees Leo looking out of the boat. A few, rogue rays of the setting sun cause a yellowish-red patch of his beard to glow.

THE FISHERMAN OPERATING THE tour, a black-haired man in flip-flops and an American football cap, switches the motor off and makes his way to the group of snorkellers who sit and lean against the sides of the ship in varying states of exhaustion. He performs a head count. "I have twenty-five written, and I see you are twenty-four."

An American sitting nearby says, "After we boarded, I heard twenty-four."

"Is that right?"

The woman with her hand on the man's thigh says, "I think I heard that too."

"Okay." The tour operator turns back into the small room that houses the steering wheel. Soon, the motor starts again.

Leo and his double both hear and don't hear the conversation. They are the only tourists still standing, peering out at the reef they're leaving. They look out at the waters, empty save for the fins of sharks, tips that emerge like blemishes in an otherwise dark ocean.

ANGELS LANDING

THE SIGN AT THE trailhead read: *Since 2006, 6 have died falling from cliffs on this route.*

Paul, my husband, gazed at it. "Gotta love America, the land of lawsuits."

"What's a lawsuit?" asked my eight-year-old, Sam. She gazed up at the path, which wove upward through the canyons of Zion Park.

"Nothing." I busied myself with my backpack, checking that I had included both water bottles. "You two go ahead," I told Paul.

LAST NIGHT, THE HOTEL attendant had brought us extra blankets. "Cold, isn't it?" he asked.

"That it is," Paul said.

Sam was bouncing on the pullout bed. "We're going to Angels Landing."

The attendant, his eyes baggy and his hotel golf shirt half untucked, said, "Oh, honey, that's not for kids."

"Paul," I said.

"Anna, we've talked about this."

"Did you know only an angel can land on it?" Sam hiccupped between jumps, her white-blonde hair flying and settling.

The attendant swivelled back to Sam. "I have heard the story, yes."

"Angels don't exist," she said.

"I hear there's a chain up there for hikers to hold on to," Paul said.

I said, "My husband is an adventurous kind of person."

"From what I hear, there is a sort of handhold," commented the attendant.

"You've never been?"

"Lord, no. I'm here for the seasonal."

When the attendant left, Paul asked me, "Do you want to cancel?"

"No, no, it's fine."

"You always get like this."

Worry is an enemy I know intimately, one I can never quite keep at bay. When Sam was little, I followed her around to the point that at parties, Paul would tell people that I climbed right up on the play structures with our daughter. My anxiety was such back then that I would often half-joke about taking something prescriptive. He would get irritated and tell me that too many people already walk about drugged in this world.

Truth was, when it came to Angels Landing, I couldn't distinguish between things I should be anxious about and things unworthy of my trepidation. I also didn't want to disappoint him, especially because although the hike wasn't my idea, I had eventually agreed to it. My pride was at stake, and maybe Paul's affection for me as well. Whenever he went off alone on his wilderness trips, I was afraid of what kinds of thoughts he might be having, so far from us.

Sam had stopped jumping and was now climbing into Paul's empty suitcase. "Daddy, can you zip me up?"

"Wow, you fit right in there," I said.

"Can you believe that guy?" Paul said. "Surrounded by beauty he's never seen!"

"It does seem crazy."

"Sam, let that be a lesson to you. Do not be that guy."

"I won't." Her voice was muffled from inside the suitcase.

THE BEGINNING OF THE trail was paved, and my feet hit the pavement with a hard clop. I could still taste the artificial waffle syrup from our chain hotel's breakfast. As we hiked, I recognized the cottonwoods that our national park bus driver had pointed out as he drove us to the trailhead. Pines filled the air with a green, coniferous scent. There was also another smell, rich and caramel, which compelled me to take deep, gulping breaths.

We walked up the switchbacks. To our left was the face of

the Angels Landing formation, heating up in the sun. Sweat pooled in my armpits, so I took off my long-sleeved lightweight top. Paul and Sam — who had walked so far ahead I could only make out Sam's red knapsack — suddenly spun around and made their way back toward me. As they approached, Sam called out, "We wanted to enjoy the view with you, Mom!"

The three of us gathered at the edge of the path, separated from the drop-off by a low stone wall. I could smell Paul's two-day-old cologne; he never showered during hiking trips. He put his arm around my neck and I felt his warmth. Below us and to our right was the Virgin River, a ribbon of grey water with small foaming white crests. From up here, the cottonwoods looked like denuded broccoli bunches. Beyond the river rose rust-red cliffs covered with dark-green mossy foliage.

"Isn't it beautiful, Mom?"

"Gorgeous."

Paul shaded his eyes. "Peregrines. I had no idea they were around here."

The Zion Park bird circled upward toward a cerulean sky, and our family of three watched it until it disappeared.

TEN YEARS AGO, PAUL took me to the Bruce Trail. I had only known him for six weeks, but already I knew I could never go back to the solitariness of my life before meeting him, a life in which I hadn't even realized how lonely I'd been. That day, we hiked up to a small cliff overlooking a sea of cedars and sugar maples. Over the tree tops, a bird of prey circled.

Paul shaded his eyes with his hand then, too. "A peregrine, I think."

"How do you know?"

"I give to the Peregrine Foundation."

"You do?" He had an X-ray technician's salary, which as far as I knew he saved for travel. I'd never met anyone with an appreciation of nature before, let alone someone who gave money to a cause.

"You need to actively preserve beauty when you see it." Suddenly, Paul opened his arms wide, as if to embrace it. "The world is a fantastic place, isn't it?" He then told me that, as a result of his father's death at a young age, he had resolved to live life well.

I felt something new, a yearning to go beyond the confines of my life and embrace new experiences. I felt confidence in Paul, as if he could lead me through a new world safely. As if I could use his attitude like a tightrope across a dangerous landscape.

AT NOON, WE STOPPED in the coolness of a canyon which, according to Paul's trail map, was aptly named Refrigerator Canyon. There were a few puddles scattered among the boulders, and the air smelled damp. We sat on cold rocks and picnicked. Sam finished her lunch and ran away from us, bouncing from one wall of the canyon to the other like a moth trapped in a room. Once, she called us over to show us what she had found in a crevice in the wall: a grey exoskeleton the size of my thumb. Impossible to tell what kind of being it was, and whether it had crawled in the crevice to die or been killed because it had been too tightly wedged.

We made our way through the canyon, Sam ahead of us. At one point, she slipped off a rock and crashed on her bottom. Her cry echoed off the walls. "Owchees!"

"Hey, be careful up there!" My heart beat slightly faster.

"You okay, trooper?" Paul called out.

She dusted herself off. "I'm fine!"

When she was six, she had fallen from monkey bars. She screamed and showed a wild disarray of feelings I'd never before witnessed from her. I knelt beside her in the playground sand, saw that greyish bone had burst through her pink skin. All I could think of was what I'd been taught in a first aid course twenty years before, which was that in situations like that you were supposed to ask someone's name.

After, I banned her from the monkey bars. Paul mildly protested, and then let me have my way.

WE EXITED THE CANYON into the searing sun. Again we stripped down to our t-shirts. The trail became steep. Crooked trees bent over an increasingly perilous chasm.

Paul stayed beside me. "Are you okay?"

"Fine."

"Do your mantra."

In times of stress, I would repeat a mantra — a recommendation from my psychiatrist, who I was seeing regularly on Paul's advice. The idea was to block out negative thoughts by bombarding them with positive ones.

"I know. I just need a little space."

We stopped to catch our breaths under the umbrage of the cliff. Sam, who didn't look tired at all, leaned against the rock face. On her left calf was a streak of red dirt. Her baseball cap hid some of her face, so that it showed only the delicate line of her lips and half a flushed cheek. Leaning there, so insouciant, she looked older than her eight years.

A woman with a baby in a carrier on her back came up the trail behind us. Her baby, fat and healthy-looking, wore a blue sun hat with a tiny piece of fabric that hung down over his neck. The woman, in her mid-thirties with blonde hair tucked under a wide-brimmed hat, wore her socks folded over her sturdy hiking boots.

I had had a carrier like that for Sam, but never wore it. I didn't like that I couldn't see her face, nor could I bear to see her precariously balanced on Paul's shoulders.

"Good for you," Paul called out to the hiker as she passed.

She half turned. "Gotta take him with me, right?"

"Absolutely!"

She continued striding uphill from us, her calves freckled and brown.

IN JULY OF LAST year, the wife of one of Paul's friends had put on a garden party. I'd gone inside to get a drink while Paul mingled in the backyard, and when I came back, he was talking to a woman in cut-offs and hiking sandals.

"That sounds great!" Paul was saying.

"What?" I smiled at them and handed Paul a beer.

The woman said, "A four-day bike trip, through Quebec." She was makeup-less and her brown hair hung uncombed to her shoulders.

"With her whole family."

"One kid on his own, one on a trailer with my husband, and one on my bike."

"Three?" I asked. "How do you keep from dying of worry?"

She gave a short laugh. "I try to keep the demons at bay by ignoring them."

"We're going to do a midwestern American trip this summer," Paul said.

"The Grand Canyon?"

"Zion National Park, in Utah."

"I've had my eye on that part of the world."

"I'm trying to persuade my wife to do Angels Landing."

"Is that the one with the chain? I've heard it's incredible."

"Oh, we'll do it," I said.

Paul stared at me. "We are?"

"Oh yes. Absolutely." I took his arm, the one with which he held the beer, and felt his bicep pulsing. I smiled at her.

Another woman sidled up to us. "Is Summer telling you about her bike trip? I just love you parents who don't let children get in the way of adventure."

"That bike trip sounds crazy good," Paul said.

"Oh, you two," said the woman. I didn't know whether she was referring to Summer and her husband, or to me and Paul, or to Summer and Paul. "You put us to shame."

Looking back, I'm pretty sure that nothing was going on

then between Summer and Paul — that he, like me, had met Summer for the first time that day. They weren't together then. They must have reconnected much later, sometime after Angels Landing. And I have only myself to blame.

AFTER FIVE HOURS, WE arrived at Scout's Lookout, a salmon-coloured, sandy saddle overlooking a canyon. A few denuded pines and thorny bushes grew here and there. Pinkish slabs of rock led up to the lookout. Scattered families picnicked and took photos. I recognized another family of three we saw on the bus. They sat on the sand, plastic sandwich bags spread out at their feet.

We climbed up the rough-hewn steps and made for the edge overlooking the chasm. Directly in front of us was Angels Landing, a jagged, undulating red snake whose head was turned away from us. On top grew a few pine trees, barer than the ones on Scout's Lookout. On both sides of the jutting rock were deep chasms, and down below were masses of green trees. It was the angel's territory.

I had a sudden vision of an angel standing on the head of the snake, wrestling with Sam. In my mind's eye, I saw Sam slipping over the edge.

Paul turned to me. "What?"

"Nothing."

The dad from the other family came up behind us. He was a large man with a goofy grin and sweat on his upper lip. "Do you mind taking a picture of us?"

I moved away from the cliff. "Against the view?"

"Helen! Come take a photo!"

His wife and daughter, both slightly chubby, gathered in front of the canyon. The little girl's forehead had a band of pink on it from her sunhat, which hung around her neck. Her smile was forced.

The dad nodded to me. "Thanks. You want one too?"

"Good idea!" Paul said. He put his arms around Sam and me, and squeezed our shoulders. "I've got both of you."

I tried not to think of the drop behind us.

Paul looked at the man's daughter. "How're you enjoying the mountain?"

"It's okay," the girl said.

"She's tired," her mother said.

"She did great." The man gave me back my camera and addressed Paul. "Not doing Angels Landing, are ya?"

"Sure are."

A look of longing came over the man's face.

His wife rolled her eyes at me, before looking directly at her husband. "Don't get ideas!"

"What's your strategy with your young lady?" the man asked.

"I'm gonna hitch her to me."

"They've got ropes, Helen," the man explained.

"Good, honey. You can plan for next time."

"Have you noticed that kids have no fear?" Paul said.

The man nodded. "Sure. My legs were shaking but Kathy, she just about ran up."

"Gotta envy that, eh?"

"Take advantage of it."

AT THE TOP WAS a sign identical to the one that stood at the head of the trail: *Since 2006, 6 people have died.*

Now that we were committed, I wanted to get it over with. It would be a while before we attempted anything risky again, and there would be some time for me to breathe in some relief.

Paul pulled out Sam's tiny harness, which fit between her legs and around her waist, and started knotting the cord attached to it. Sam stepped a few metres away and stared over the chasm.

"How you folks doing?" A man had emerged seemingly from nowhere, though possibly he'd been behind a bush. He had a wide-brimmed hat and a khaki uniform.

Paul looked up, his hands still working on his knot. "Fantastic day, isn't it?"

"Folks, the path is off-limits today."

Paul's hands stilled. "This one?"

"The path's washed out."

Paul looked over at Sam, who was standing on a boulder overlooking the canyon, bouncing on her toes. "Sam, get down!" He turned to the ranger. "Is it really a problem or is it, you know, rules being rules?"

"Paul," I said.

The ranger stared at Paul. "We don't recommend the hike for kids under sixteen."

"We have ropes."

"Fact is the path is closed." He took a bottle out from a hook on his belt and took a swig.

Paul's body vibrated, as if he were a large cat ready to pounce.

Sam skipped up to us and I crouched down. Though I was annoyed on Paul's behalf by the ranger's ambivalence to his disappointment, I was also relieved. I tried to keep the elation out of my voice when I told her, "The trail isn't open today, hon. It's too wet."

"Dad!"

Paul turned around.

"Sorry," said the ranger.

"Whatever."

Paul moved at a brisk pace, back toward Scout's Lookout, and we followed him. As Sam tried to catch up to him, she kept saying, "But we have ropes!"

We came to the lookout as the other family was packing up their gear. The father looked up from tying his knapsack. "You all changed your mind?"

Paul gave a noncommittal wave and quickened his pace. His shoulders were hitched up to his ears as he crossed the plateau.

I felt sad for him. Paul believed obstacles were meant to be scaled, and he always scaled them. All except this one. My relief, however, was greater than my pity. I imagined a figure dancing a jig on top of a mountain.

After about twenty minutes, Paul slowed down, allowing me to catch my breath. Sam was a few metres ahead of us now, still sulking, studiously not talking to us.

Paul gave a low chuckle. "Oh well, all's for the best. I was afraid we'd have to carry you out of there." He smiled at me, and I smiled back.

The heat was letting up as we started back down the switchbacks. Some shadows hung over the path, and I could feel the day's sweat drying, my body cooling off. We stopped for a pee break. On one side of the path were the cliffs; on the other, some step-like plateaus covered with crumbling boulders and thorny bushes. While we waited for Sam, Paul and I wandered over to the edge of the cliff, looking at the view. Beside us was a juniper tree. I could tell because there had been a picture in the park's guide map. The tree was dying; it was split down the middle, having been struck by lightning. Marshmallow-white berries hung like earrings from its branches. Paul broke off a small branch and brought it to me. "Smell." From it came the caramel scent that had followed us since earlier that day.

We sat down on crackling, dead pine branches. I put my head on Paul's shoulder and dozed for a few seconds. Later, I would see this moment as a kind of stasis in the life of our family — a snapshot of what might have been had we stayed together: Paul and Sam blocked from doing the things that terrified me, and no one could blame me for it. Our family reunited through being thwarted. Years later, first when an acquaintance told me that Paul and Summer were living together, and then when Sam turned sixteen and left me to live with her father, this was this moment that I mourned: Paul and I waiting, together, for Sam to return to us.

My eyes flew open. "Where's Sam?"

Behind the boulders, on the slope, were crumpled toilet paper and a smell of urine.

Paul called her name, and his voice echoed.

"I'm going to kill her." I followed him back up the mountain. Soon, sweat was accumulating again between my shoulder blades. I was breathing heavily. "You go ahead."

All those things that you imagine when you have kids nagged at me. Those visions that wake you at three in the morning. You picture your child hit by a car or stung by a thousand bees. Or falling. Those thoughts were there, but I wouldn't let them in. I started making deals with God. *I won't do these crazy trips anymore*, I told him. I felt ridiculous engaging in that kind of negotiation, but I also hoped that God existed and that he heard me.

It seemed to take twice as long as before to go back up to Scout's Lookout. At first I could see Paul bounding ahead of me, taking the path at a light jog, as if he were doing some cross-country running, but soon I couldn't see him anymore.

AS I APPROACHED SCOUT'S Lookout, I could make out people scattered on the plateau. I squinted hard to discern my husband and daughter among them. After a few seconds, two figures detached themselves from the others, and I recognized the red of Sam's backpack.

Paul led her toward me with his hand on her shoulder. Sam's hair lifted and fell in the wind, the braid that I had made in the morning having come undone. I sniffed hard and wiped my nose with the back of my hand.

"Mom! I climbed it!"

"You think she's kidding." Paul moved beside me and placed a hand on my neck. I sniffed again and took out a tissue from the pocket of my hiking pants. Sam looked at me and squirmed, but she also smiled, as if she couldn't help it.

"Where's the ranger?" I asked Sam.

She shrugged. "Not sure. Anyways, it really wasn't hard."

"That was not smart," Paul said.

"There are so going to be consequences," I said.

"You should not put your mother through something like that."

"And her father," I said. "What about her father?"

"We're going," Paul declared, and led us toward the path that would take us back down the mountain. I glanced back once at the fork in the paths and saw the ranger hitching up his pants. He seemed to be rushing toward us, moving his arm as if to call us back.

"Let's go." I couldn't vouch for keeping my temper with the ranger. Couldn't he do his damned job?

We practically ran down the switchbacks, saying nothing to one another. As I galloped, anger gave way to rage, a fury beyond my control. I wasn't angry at Sam anymore, but at Paul. Sam would not have taken this risk had Paul not encouraged her.

When we stopped for water, Paul asked, "Sam, was it amazing?"

"It was pretty cool. But I wasn't looking down very much. I was holding on to the chain."

"Jesus Christ, Paul." My words came out in a kind of strangle.

When the park shuttle picked us up, we collapsed on seats apart from one another. After a while, Sam came to sit beside Paul. She put her head on his lap and fell asleep, her head bouncing with every pothole.

ONCE WE GOT BACK to our hotel room, my anger — directed again at Sam — returned in full force, and I started to mete out some punishments. I felt like someone fiddling with a pressure cooker, letting off little bursts of steam so as not to let the whole thing blow. "If you think you're going on another hike tomorrow, forget it."

"Well," Paul said.

I said nothing. I went into the bedroom.

Later, as Sam was taking a shower, Paul came in and said, "This is getting ridiculous."

"Seriously?" I paced back and forth between the living room and our bedroom.

He followed me into the living room. "Point is, nothing happened."

"Something could have!"

"Do you want to be like that guy, that hotel guy? Don't you want to live for real, not just exist?"

"That has nothing to do with it. Sam could've been hurt."

"Children who don't take risks become risk-averse adults. Like all those things you ban her from doing. Monkey bars, roller coasters. And crossing the street by herself. She's almost nine!"

I stared. "Why don't you tell me when you don't agree with my parenting, then?"

"I do, but you don't really hear."

The reality was that he couldn't promise me that nothing bad would actually happen in the future. And something stubborn was growing in me, something tied to my inborn caution.

Sam, in pyjamas, tiptoed into the bedroom. I was now sitting on an armchair, looking out the wide hotel window onto an enormous parking lot. She kissed me on the cheek and said goodnight. She smelled of the hotel's cheap shampoo.

Paul undressed in silence and slipped into bed. Soon he was asleep, snoring lightly in the diminishing light of the spring evening.

I sat until the sun set, stripes of orange and red and mauve and then, finally, tar black. A glare came from the fluorescent parking lot lights. I could make out Sam's hair, fanned out on her pillow, and her long eyelashes closed over her green eyes.

I rose and started packing. All the while, my husband and my daughter slept. I started with my suitcase, then tiptoed into the living room and packed Sam's suitcase. As I packed, my anger gave way to sadness. Some being, other than me, I had tried to fend off for a long time, was winning. Whatever lay dormant in me had a personality of its own and could not join my husband and daughter in their search for, what? Whether it was risk or adventure, I still couldn't make up my mind.

I SAW PAUL IN a grocery store the other day. I don't normally shop there, I had just decided to stop for groceries after an appointment in the western end of the city.

Paul was in the freezer section. His cheeks seemed slightly more hollowed than the last time I'd seen him, his hairline more receded. In the cart next to him was a child of about three years. He had overgrown brown hair, and the same green-speckled-with-brown eyes as Paul. For a moment I couldn't move. *Sam knows about his child*, I thought. *Why hasn't she told me?*

Paul was reading a box he held in his left hand. With his right hand, he was playing a game of pushing the cart away from him, then letting it go, then stretching his arm to catch it again. Each time he pushed it away, the child squealed.

I heard a clip-clop of heels, and a woman approached Paul and the child. Although she was wearing work clothes, and her forehead was more lined than it had been at the garden party, I recognized Summer easily. She placed a hand on the cart. "Where were you guys? I couldn't find you any-where. You know I hate when you go off without a word."

He smiled at her, his eyes crinkling in the way I remem-bered. My nose pricked, despite my satisfaction at reading worry in her. This was quickly replaced by pity, and then sympathy, which alleviated my chronic loneliness, if only for a few seconds. I pivoted on my heels, preparing to walk away as quickly as possible without seeming rushed. I hoped she hadn't recognized me.

"We were here all this time," Paul said.

The Bread Maker

SANDRA DOESN'T MENTION THE discoloration on her son's jaw, though she feels the bruise as a tightening under her own clavicle. It's like when Glen was little and the boys would take against him, for no reason that she could see, and she was powerless to do anything about it.

In the past she would have said something, straight out, about the bruise. That changed the last time he came home. She'd asked about his injuries right away and he yelled at her, crashed out the door, didn't call her for months, and then after that only *hi* and *how-are-you* and *how's-the-weather-*type conversations. All because she couldn't bear to see him beaten up again.

He walks past her and toward the kitchen at the back of the house. Following him, she notices with surprise that there is a pale wedge on the top of his head, at the part, where his long, light-brown hair is starting to thin prematurely.

"Glen, what are you doing here?"

"Anything to eat?"

She moves quickly — tripping in her slippered feet, but recovering herself — and grabs the back of his shirt before he enters the kitchen. "Wait. I'll get it."

"Thanks, Mom."

Her eyes widen at his thanks, but she says only, "Why don't you wait in the living room?"

As he walks away, she tenses. She has nothing in the fridge. Or next to nothing. She kneads the pinch at the back of her neck with both hands and then begins scrounging for something to eat. After staring at the near-empty fridge for a while, she takes out a piece of old cheddar and, gouging out a few craters of mold, she brings the rectangle to her nose. Sharp, but still okay. Using the same knife, which he had bought her with his grocery store money when he was eleven, she carves off some slices. Then she pulls out her fancy crackers, the thin ones with sesame seeds and honeycomb latticework, and puts everything on a chipped white plate: cheese on one side, crackers on the other.

When she enters the living room he's sitting on the only chair in the room, the one with the orange plastic seat that she found on the lawn of the school when they were renovating.

His legs are propped up. "What happened to the other one?"

She blinks at what has been her table for the past few months, a sheet of particleboard on two crates. "I sold it."

"Really?"

"I needed a change."

She looks around, trying to decide if she should keep standing or if he'll consider it hovering. "Here." She hands him the plate, and catches a sour scent from her right armpit. She hasn't washed in a couple of days. There's no one to wash for, and not showering saves on her hot water bills. These days she only showers before her shifts at WellLife retirement home — and after the government cutbacks, after the union protected the old employees, the ones older than her, she hasn't had regular shifts for ten months. She hopes Glen doesn't notice the smell.

He chomps down on the crackers, bits scattering. She feels a rush of anger for the waste. Why does he have to eat them so fast? Soon it will be saltines only, with their sawdust texture that leaves a sour taste in her mouth.

She's on tenterhooks, not wanting to ask him again why he's there.

As if reading her mind, he says, "I missed home."

Which is bullshit. The minute he turned twelve, he began shutting her out. He would leave the house after school and come back hours later stinking of pot. At sixteen he left for Vancouver, as far west as he could possibly go and still get free healthcare. To get away from her, he'd have gone straight into the ocean if he could.

He swallows, starts coughing a bit.

"I'll get you some water," she says. When she returns, he downs the water in a few gulps. She makes to take the glass from him, but he holds it tightly to himself.

"I'll get it, Mom." He continues to sit there, though. "Haven't been baking lately?"

"Not lately."

"That's a shame."

She doesn't know what to say to that, either. He hated her whole-wheat rolls, wanted store-bought white bread. Maybe he liked her cannoli, though. The ones she made when he was a child. The last time would have been on his eleventh birthday; the year after, they fought too much and out of spite she bought him a No Frills blueberry pie, with a crust that tasted like cardboard.

Sandra catches Glen studying her, and realizes she's wearing her old housecoat — the red and garish Chinatown one she once gave to her mother for Christmas, back when she had money for extras. Her mother gave it back after Robert left her the first time. She was stuck home with baby Glen then, wearing pyjamas all day, sticky with spit-up and caramel-smelling formula. Now, Sandra tries to put one foot behind the other so he won't see her curling, uncut toenails.

"Not working Sundays anymore, Mom?"

"No, not anymore."

"It was mean of them to make you go on Sundays."

"It was good money." She rubs her hands. The arthritis pain has grown bad and over the past year she's developed this habit, as if by rubbing she'll rub the ache right out.

Glen catches her eye. "How're the hands?"

"Bad." She used to run a kitchen at the home. Was good at it, too. Now she's just a cook. On work days she takes an Advil, but only half, to stretch out the bottle.

"Have you seen a doctor?"

"Christ, no. I hate how they look at you, with all that pity."

He looks at her carefully. "They're just doing their job. Sometimes people just want to help."

She thinks he blushes then, or maybe it's a trick of the dimming winter light. It always gets dark early in this east-facing house. But maybe he is actually embarrassed, as if he's speaking from experience. He'd lived on the streets and then, somehow, ended up on the other side. For the last few years, he's worked helping the homeless in Vancouver's downtown east side, bringing them methadone and clean needles — surprising the heck out of her, considering how he was self-centred. Maybe that's the way it is with kids, all kids are self-centred. It's just that she's shocked at the change in him.

"I just thought of something," her son says. "Do you eat nightshades?"

"Night what?"

"Tomatoes. Eggplant. I heard they cause inflammation."

"Where'd you hear that?"

He shrugs. "People say it."

"You're just naming things you hate!" She laughs, like the old days when they used to joke together.

"Actually, I've been eating vegetarian. It's so crunchy granola out there."

"Holy moly. What the heck is that?"

He ignores her, so she taunts him a little more, trying to get him laughing with her. "No B on B?" Their name for bologna on bread.

"Do you know how they make that stuff?" He uses words like *nitrites* and *nitrosamines*, and she loses the thread of what he's saying. He's always been smart, always good with words. As he talks, hope rises in her, seeing as now he's noticing her in a way he wasn't before: as a real person, with feelings and needs and wants. Now, he is *interested*.

She interrupts his processed-meat talk. "Glen, how long're you staying?"

He nods as if he's been waiting for her. "I was thinking of coming home."

"What about work?"

"I'm gonna take a break."

"You going back to school?"

"What? No."

She thinks about it for a few seconds. "You're not becoming one of those Buddhists, are you?"

"Nothing like that. Although it's not so bad, you know."

He paces, goes to the window, and parts the greying muslin curtain. "I thought the area was gentrifying."

"Some say that."

"Look, to tell you the truth, I quit."

"Oh."

She's not sure if she's relieved or angry, or maybe both. What will they do for money? All of a sudden she can't breathe, seized by her memories of the early years when she didn't know how she would provide for Glen, until the job at WellLife — with benefits and, for the first time, a feeling of being good at something. That time she made tomato sauce from scratch, discovering there was something beyond the eat-sleep-earn cycle.

"Why'd you quit, Glen?"

"Maybe I was sick of being beaten up."

He sounds mocking, but when she looks at him she sees some pain behind his eyes. Maybe it's the sting of failure, of wanting to give when no one wants to take. She knows that feeling well, from raising Glen. Now, when she could use some help, she wishes he'd turn some of that helping attention to her.

Glen lifts an eyebrow at her. "Aren't you happy I'm home?"

"Yes, I am! I am." She rushes toward him and then, catching a whiff of her sour scent, stops short. "Maybe you could look for something here."

"For sure!" he says. He rises and, shock of shock, takes his dishes with him. She hears him clattering in the kitchen. "Where's your broom, Mom?"

"What for?"

"Crumbs."

She follows his gaze toward the floor, the dots like sowbugs rolling around. They might as well join the dustballs that rise and settle whenever the wind blows, she thinks. "In the lean-to?" she muses, and he goes to look.

She used to be house-proud, back when Robert first

bought the place and fixed it up, pounding the baseboards back in and painting the walls and ceilings. He even got an electrician friend to replace the knob-and-tube wiring that was part-and-parcel of these old Victorians. Sandra mopped the hardwood floors with vinegar and dusted the oak mantelpiece. She loved the high ceilings; after living in her grandparents' bungalow her whole life, she felt she could breathe.

When Robert's handiwork didn't come in anymore and he got depressed and took it out on her, she took over the maintenance. She plastered the hole in the hallway that he had kicked in, washed his vomit off the toilet's base. She kept herself up in the same way, shaving her legs and dyeing her roots with Clairol. And when Rob went away for good, she continued to love the house. She used to thank God that he didn't fight her for the place — no doubt he knew he'd lose that battle.

She's stopped cleaning, now that she couldn't afford her mortgage. She felt deflated, just gave up. But every once in a while, she gets sick of herself and her house and she washes the counters and mops the floors, and gives herself a good scouring. Then she looks at the elegant hardwood, and the Victorian ceilings that awed her when Robert first brought her here, and she cries and asks her house for forgiveness.

Glen comes back from the kitchen with a straw broom and dustpan. She watches, astonished, as he bends over like a stem and sweeps up his crumbs. He leaves again and she hears him hitting the pan against her metal trashcan.

"Hey, Mom, what happened to The Beast?"

She'd forgotten the name he'd given to her bread maker, back when he was little. "It's in the shop." She's glad he can't see her face. The bread maker is a Braun. A sturdy brand. Good thing Glen doesn't know that it's impossible to break a machine like that.

He comes back in and smiles. "Remember how the kids used to beat me up for bringing in your whole wheat rolls?"

"I had no idea."

"Water under the bridge." He pauses for a moment, thinking. "Hey, you're not becoming a minimalist, are you?"

She rubs her hands again, suddenly aware that maybe it's a nervous habit.

He continues. "Although some say it's good for you. Very Zen. I know someone who sold all her things to hike the West Coast trail, and she said —"

"Excuse me," Sandra says. She goes to the bathroom so he won't see her cry, and takes a bit longer on the toilet than necessary. The familiarity of the bathroom calms her down. It looks the same as it always has, with a woven basket containing her plastic nail brush and pharmacy-brand hand cream, and her pink toothbrush in a plastic cup on the sink. One time, after he beat her, Robert bought her a purse. She should have sold it, but she got so mad that she dumped it in the garbage bin.

The bread maker. What a story. She had won the bread maker at one of WellLife's annual fundraising lotteries, when she was a new employee. She read the manual that came with it at least ten times, then bought flour and yeast, made dough, and after the first failures, made a round loaf, as airy and delicious as anything she'd ever eaten, including her grandmother's sponge cake.

That was only the beginning. She went to the library and got some cookbooks, all Italian, in memory of her grandmother, who wasn't Italian, but had gone to Rome on a holy pilgrimage. Sandra could only afford discounted vegetables and cheap cuts of meats, but still, she was hooked. Her favourite dish to make was carbonara, which she made with one egg instead of four, and one slice of ham instead of three.

Later, when her boss was away, she made a giant pot of homemade spaghetti sauce for WellLife's residents. Her boss was furious and yelled at her about the two hundred dollars' worth of tomatoes she'd squandered. But after he calmed down, he leaned forward in his swivel chair and confessed that one of the residents had liked the sauce, praising it to her mother, a patron. When the kitchen manager quit, her boss promoted Sandra in her place.

All this, because she had brought the bread maker home — and only because she thought she could resell it. She never did, until now. It was the last thing to go, after the heirloom table and the sofa she had bought with her first paycheck.

When Sandra returns from the bathroom, Glen has removed his sweatshirt and is doing pushups. "Glen! Are you *exercising?*"

Her glance flits across bruises on his lower back, on his kidneys. Bruises the colour of bumblebees and violets, which puts her in mind of the garden at her grandparents' Windsor house, before the factory laid her grandfather off and he got sick and her grandmother got sad.

He grunts for two more push-ups and flies up, recoiling a little on the back of his heels. "That feels good."

Now that she's looking harder, she sees that he looks better than the last time she saw him. His skinny arms have some bulk around the biceps. Then she recalls his comment, about the *she* who sold all her belongings to go hiking the West Coast trail. "Glen, do you have...? Is there a girl?"

He smiles. "Hard to hide stuff from you."

She stares at him. So that's it. And if the past hour has shown her anything, it's that he's really fallen. That's what love does. Or certain kinds of love. The right kind makes you love yourself more. Like when Glen was eleven and a half, and she looked at him needing her, and decided she'd had enough of being her husband's doormat.

"She took care of me," Glen says. "You would love her, Mom."

Just like Glen, to be so keen about something. Until his passion gets squeezed out like a J-Cloth being wrung out. Sandra hopes that this interest will last. Silently, she praises the girl who's taken her son off the streets.

"Mind if I take a shower?" He's off, taking the stairs two by two like he always did. A minute later, he calls down, "There's no hot water!"

A month ago her neighbour told her to turn off the hot water when she's not using it, to save money. She won't know if he's right until the next bill.

Before she has time to make something up, Glen is already galloping down the basement stairs to turn it back on. Five seconds later he whizzes by her. "I'll shave while I wait. Do you have any razors?"

"Try under the sink!" she yells up. "If it's rusty don't use it!"

For a few moments, she's elated by his energy. But as she stands in the doorway of the living room, she again wonders how she's going to hide the facts from him. "Woohoo!" she hears from above, a sign that the water is still cold. She listens to hear if he's going to turn it back off, but he doesn't, and she sits down on the hard plastic chair, which after a while hurts her lower back.

He brings the smell of cheap soap and shaving lotion down with him. "Here, I have something for you. Jenny made it."

It's a circular cap, knit in garish colours. Suddenly Sandra can picture the girl. A waif with long, blonde hair. A hippie. She starts to laugh. No way she'll wear that hat. She'll give it to Old Kingsley at WellLife, on her next shift. Then she remembers that it will be a long while until her next shift.

"I was thinking we could move in with you, if that's cool."

"Here?"

"She likes cooking. You could hang together!"

So he wants a home, then. First the girl, then the nest. Like how Sandra got pregnant soon after meeting Robert, way back. How he went out and started a contracting business and bought this old Victorian with good bones.

It seems to her that her family has always been about good bones. Trouble is, sometimes bones get broken, and even if you fix them, they don't seem to stay fixed. Like they've been weakened too much and won't be again what they used to be.

"How long before you go back?" Sandra asks.

"We're not going back," Glen says. "She's here, in the city, at her parents' house. Did I tell you that she's from here too?"

"Can't you stay at her parents' place?"

"Not a chance. Her parents are nuts. Mom, do you not want us here?"

"Of course I do." She's doing the calculations, trying to see the situation from all angles. Maybe if she tells him about the house, he'll be able to help her figure out how to make some cash, enough to — she keeps doing this, she realizes. Trying to recoup what has already been lost.

"We'll be in the basement. You won't see us at all," says Glen.

"I guess we can figure it out."

"Thanks, Mom." The "thanks" seems perfunctory, as if he assumed she'd say yes. Of course she would. And now she has. What has she agreed to? Where will they go when the house is gone? Yet, her heart swells briefly at the thought of having him under her roof again, of smelling his cheap shaving cream waft into the kitchen in the mornings, of serving him his Cheerios. He comes toward her and bends down to embrace her, his hands briefly touching her back. When he releases her, his nose is wrinkled. "Why don't you sit down," Glen says, frowning at her.

"I'm all right."

"No, sit down." He helps her lower herself in it. She doesn't tell him that, at fifty-five, she's not an old lady needing help. But maybe she is, after all. In the bathroom mirror she'll catch a glimpse of herself, with her sleepy eyelids, and her mouth puckered from too much smoking, and see her own mother. He goes into the kitchen and she hears the suck of the fridge door opening. "You really have nothing. We can go out to eat. You working later?"

Has he already forgotten?

"No!" she calls out from the living room.

She wonders how long it will take before the bank seizes the house. She's been waiting for the past ten months. Have they forgotten about her? Maybe there's a chance she'll be able to keep it. But she knows the bank will come. The people in charge always come when there's something they want. Not like the years nobody came to visit or to help, when they looked the other way.

Glen comes back in. "Mom, get dressed. We'll go for pizza."

"I really don't feel like it, Glen. I'm tired."

"Fair enough. I'll get us takeout. No, wait. I'll get Jenny and then I'll get takeout. You'll love her, I swear." He goes out the front door and she feels a blast of winter air, whip-cold and metallic.

Maybe, if the house gets taken, her boss would let her stay at WellLife. But no, there aren't any rooms even for would-be residents, and won't be for years to come.

There's a noise and frosty air and Glen is back. "Mom, you have any cash? I'm out." He doesn't even look ashamed, just like his old twelve-year-old self wouldn't.

She's already reaching for her synthetic handbag when she remembers that her wallet is empty. "I'm sorry, Glen. Haven't had time to go to the bank."

"Okay, no worries. I'll ask Jenny. See ya."

He runs out the door. The inner door closes on its hinges with a protesting squeak, as if the house were a living, breathing thing, reluctant to let one of its occupants go. Sandra wants to cry. For her lost dreams and for what seems right now like the end of the line for her family. She wants to weep for unspoken things, for things Glen hasn't said to her. That he loves her. That he's forgiven her for her mistakes, for letting Robert beat her, for giving Robert up to the cops.

But still, Glen has come home. He's in love and he's different and he's come home, and maybe, just maybe, love will make him stick. She thinks about bread: how she never knows if the yeast is going to take, if the bread is going to rise. It's labour and it's luck; and no one can tell you if it will work out.

ON THE TRAIN TO ANTIBES

WHEN I WAS SEVENTEEN, I met a guy named Ames on the
train between Paris and Antibes. I was in a corridor, looking
out at the unfurling landscape of telephone wires, coniferous
trees, and yellow square houses with grey tiles the shape of
tears. He paused opposite me and leaned against the glass.
After a few seconds, he lifted his head, having found out that
if you rested too long against the window, the rattling glass
would bruise your temple. "*Vous êtes seule?*"

"*Oui.*"

"Ah, American."

"Canadian. But I speak French."

He introduced himself, pronouncing his name with a short
a that sounded like the *o* in the word *love*. "*Tu veux prendre un
café, Jeanne?*"

"*D'accord.*"

HE LED ME THROUGH the train to a first-class dining car. There were salmon tablecloths, plush armchairs, and pink napkins folded into triangles on porcelain plates.

"You sure we're allowed to be here?"

"I have a first-class ticket. My father likes to take care of us. At least, from a distance." He asked for two coffees and two mineral waters, clearly used to ordering people around.

He had a narrow face, deep-set brown eyes, and short hair parted on the left. There was a small dent in his chin, which marred the picture, but not too much. His cologne, sweet and strong in a way I had begun to recognize, was typically French. His hands were large: they grasped the espresso cup with thumb and forefinger, leaving the rest of the fingers curled at the side of the cup like crumpled paper. He drank the coffee in one gulp.

He told me he was on his way home from an army base near Paris, after taking leave from the service to deal with an urgent family matter. It was impossible to get tickets going south in August, with everyone travelling in that direction, so his father had bribed an official to get him a ticket. "Some poor sod lost his berth."

"That's terrible."

"*Oui.*" He sounded only moderately sorry. He gestured to the waiter and pointed to his empty cup. "And you? You're on a trip to discover yourself? No, no, don't be angry. *Je plaisante.* I'm glad I met you."

The anger that had driven me to leave home was beginning to dissipate, leaving in its place an emptiness which I filled with brief sexual encounters. I'd already slept with several guys since starting my trip two months earlier. In Amsterdam I walked the canals and smoked pot with a fellow traveller. At one point, I leaned against a canal wall and let my companion, a redhead from Britain, lick my ear. I gauged that my transition to fearless adventuress was really taking hold at that moment, and as his tongue circled the seashell of the inside of my ear, I closed my eyes. Since then I'd slept with Dutch, Belgians, French, and a Senegalese who was visiting his sister in Paris. Sex was losing its novelty. I was getting bored.

The train car's sliding doors hissed open and a tall, thin woman walked in. Her auburn hair, done up in a bun, accentuated her high rouged cheekbones, and her eyes were almond shaped, Slavic-looking. She clip-clopped past us on high heels. "*Un café, s'il vous plaît,*" she said as she sat down. She opened a briefcase and began marking up some papers with a red pen.

She reminded me of my sixteen-year-old sister Maddie, who always acted as if the rest of us didn't exist. During our worst moments, I blamed my parents for her narcissism. She would draw them to her as if she were a flame and they the moths, and I would feel left behind. But did my mother favour my sister? I don't know: nobody calibrates parental attention as carefully as an unhappy sibling does. I have no children of my own. I don't want to be tied down to anything. But I am the godmother to two girls. The eldest is so precocious that it would take serious effort not to be enthralled by her — and the younger one already seems to teeter on the edge of understanding that people judge her differently from her sister.

"What I love about French women is that they take themselves in hand," said Ames. "American women, they don't know what they want." He drank his mineral water, quickly emptying it. "What's wrong? Don't take it personally. I'm sure you know what you're doing." He put his hand on my forearm. "Let's go smoke *du shit*."

I had never heard the expression he used. "Pot?"

"Shhh." His hand on my arm was warm. He leaned in. "It will help."

WE PASSED THROUGH THE train all the way to a car at the opposite end. The luggage was stored in cages on raised platforms. The noise of the tracks was loud.

"No one will come here," he said.

We sat and leaned against one of the walls. I sat with my legs stretched out, the rubber floor rubbing against the back of my knees, giving me a kind of carpet burn. Ames took a small plastic baggy from his pocket and, balancing paper and pot on his thigh, rolled a joint as if he were performing a delicate operation.

Because of my sister's drug addiction, I hadn't touched anything more mind-altering than beer through high school and beyond. I smoked my first joint in Amsterdam; I figured that if I were going to start my life as an independent woman, free of any sense of filial obligation, and unravelling and remaking my identity on my own terms, I had to take risks. As risks went, pot seemed mild.

He lit the joint and inhaled, then handed it to me and watched as I puffed. "You won't get anything out of that. Why aren't you breathing it in? Inhaling — that's how you say it, right?" He took the joint back. "My mom is a nurse. At first, she was very worried. Then she did *une recherche*. Now she's okay with it. 'To each his own medicine,' she said."

Again he passed me the joint. He continued talking, but I was too engrossed in myself to listen. I inhaled more deeply, three times in a row, and waited to see what would happen. Memories appeared, cartoon figures zooming toward me like those numbers and letters on Sesame Street.

I remembered the day Maddie told our father — our gentle father, who had bathed us as babies, who had cared for us in the way of a man who always wanted daughters — that she'd had an abortion. Watching from my perch on our living room couch, where I had been reading, I concluded that she was telling him to get his attention. This was usual for her, despite the fact that he always lavished on her his devotion, even when she didn't need it. In this case, she'd already made her decision about her predicament and didn't really need him; I thought that she was trying to hurt him, only I didn't know why, except that maybe it was to cause some drama. She succeeded. Our father began feeling unwell, and by nightfall was in the hospital with angina. I saw myself in the door frame of our father's hospital room. My sister wanted in, but I was barring the door. Our mother, who was in the corridor, was trying to persuade me to bring my arms down. She had one hand on my biceps.

As usual when I considered things back home, I was angry all over again. I was also sad. I understood that we would never get better as a family, that I would always resent my sister, and that my parents would always try to bring us together.

I also felt longing — but for what I didn't know.

"*Oh là là*. Not so fast." Ames pulled my right hand down to prevent me from inhaling further, and with his other hand forced the joint out of my fingers. With his left hand, he pinned my wrist down to my thigh.

I waited for him to draw me to him, but after a minute or two, he started talking again, as though he hadn't talked to anyone before, at least not about everything in his life.

He told me about his father, a travelling businessman and a womanizer who had left the family again and again. The first time his father asked him to cover up an affair, Ames was eleven. His mother had sent him to the village pub to call his father home for dinner; there, he saw his father with a woman.

"Her collarbone was bony," he told me. "I remember because I'd always noticed my mother's collarbone, which was wide, from being Portuguese. And freckled, from gardening. This wispy girl, this girl with him, had a laugh with no confidence, you know? She didn't know what she was doing. He had his arm around her and her left hand came up to meet his hand, like a closed flower."

He drew on the joint.

"When he got home, he came into my room and put some

money on my night table. I didn't have to ask why. Well, my mother didn't ask and I didn't tell." As he talked, he bounced his hand on my thigh up and down like a jumping spider, without realizing. "Oh, I'm talking too much? Well, what do you want to do? You want a little more attention?"

His hand was back in his own lap. I shrugged and smiled, pretending to not care how things would play out. "Did I tell you my sister stole my boyfriend?"

"And you're mad?"

"It was the last straw." I said it in English, not knowing the French expression. I said it knowing the situation between Maddie and me was more complicated than I was making it sound. My sister had struggled for years with inner demons, and I felt sorry for her. I also loved her, for she was bright, talented, and kind when the impulse took her. I thought she deserved some happiness. I resented that she would receive it at my expense. It had always been that way. I tried to clarify my use of the English expression to Ames. "Lots of things for many years," I said.

"*La goutte qui fait déborder le vase.*" He gave it some thought. "I understand this last straw." He looked at me. "You're an attractive girl."

Ha, I thought. *There you go, Maddie: guys like me, too. It's not always about you.*

Ames kissed me, and my inner creature of pleasure raised its head. I put my hands around his shoulders. His lips were wet, but his tongue stayed out of my mouth. Then he drew away. He put out the roach, which he'd been holding up in the air away from us. It had burned down to his fingers. He squashed it on the floor and sighed.

"These days, I tell people what I think. Directly. Like last night. 'Do me a favour,' my father says. I said to him, 'It's the last time I'm getting you out of a mess.'"

He nodded as if he were convincing himself. Then he pulled the plastic baggy out of his pocket and opened it up.

Suddenly, the train's wheels screeched and my head slammed into the back of one of the cages.

"*Putain.*" Ames was lying half on his side, against the sliding doors.

The suitcases had held, except for a stroller that had jumped one of the elastic straps and was now lying on the floor between us. Ames eyed it, then asked me, "You okay?"

I rubbed my arm. "I think so."

He helped me up. Then he tried to open the outer door, but couldn't. There must have been an automatic mechanism that locked it in the event of an accident. It was too dark to see anything out the window. Outside, male voices were yelling. Ames stepped over the stroller and opened the sliding door to the next car.

UP AND DOWN THE sleeper cars, people in dressing gowns peered out of their rooms. We got to one of the first-class cars and found the woman from the dining room lying across the corridor floor. Her head, bent at a strange angle, rested on the baseboard. Her briefcase was at her feet.

Ames hurried to her and bent down. Blood trickled down

the woman's cheek from a cut on the right side of her head. "Help," he said to me.

I hated being someone's prop. I went to his side and took the woman's arm. Her perfume smelled of overripe cherries.

"Where is your room?" Ames asked. "*Madame?*"

Her eyes focused on a point down the hall. "*Numéro huit. La clé est dans ma poche.*"

Ames held her propped up against the wall while I reached into her business jacket, which was lined with something satiny.

Her room was the same size as mine, only with a single bed instead of two bunk beds. The bed was made with a thin white coverlet. On top was a pink peignoir, unfolded but not crumpled, as if it had been placed there lovingly, but in a rush. Gauze curtains hung over two windows. On the other side of the room a hinged table was folded open, and on it was a closed metal box with a handle, which I assumed contained makeup.

I let go of the woman, but Ames walked her to the bed, where her small frame dropped heavily and made the bedsprings squeak. She seemed softer than she had been in the dining car, blurred at the edges. Her lipstick was gone, and her eyeliner was smudged, but she was more beautiful than ever. "Could you pass a tissue?" she asked.

As if he had taken care of people all his life, Ames reached for a box next to the bed. She put the tissue to her temple and closed her eyes. "Should we call a doctor?" Ames asked. When she shook her head slowly, Ames instead brought her water from the tiny sink.

The train's intercom came on. A male voice told us there had been an accident and that, due to minor damage, we would switch trains at the next station. Anyone injured was asked to proceed to the first aid station in the last car.

"I'm okay," said the woman.

"Are you sure?" Ames frowned at her.

The woman sighed. "My husband told me he would pick me up in Paris, but I insisted on the train. I get so much work done." She smiled at me. "*Enfin*, the landscape is nice, *n'est-ce-pas?*"

"*Bon.*" He gave her his room number. "Knock on the door if you need me."

IN MY FIRST MONTH of travel, I received letters from my family. My father hoped I was enjoying the sights. My mother seemed distracted, concerned with Maddie's daily appointments and making sure she was on track. A few months before, our parents had asked me to take Maddie to my drama club and beg my director to give her an understudy position. Maddie and I had in common an affection for theatre, and I had adored putting on skits with her when we were children. I felt then that we were cut from the same cloth, that she was one of the few who really understood me. So it was natural that, after another one of Maddie's periods of drug abuse, my parents would ask me for this particular favour. But I refused, arguing that, for once, I wanted to do something that didn't involve her. I wanted them to see my point of view, to support me in a way that they never had.

They always took Maddie's side. Now, in her letter, my mother reminded me of the fact that I had not done what they asked, and that Maddie's health was worse because of it, implying that I had failed them all.

There was even a postcard from Maddie:

Dear Jeanne, I'm at home now, which sucks as you can imagine. Mom and Dad don't let me out of their sight. And everything is flat. You don't get it, I know. I'm just saying. I miss how mad you get, at least it makes some waves around here. Are you still too pissed to let me join you there, à la Owl and The Pussycat?

It was a reference to a play we had put on in our living room years before, modelled on Edward Lear's *The Owl and the Pussycat*. I was the Owl, she, the Pussycat. We married using my dad's wedding ring. At the end, we hugged, and I smelled the honey-scented shampoo we both used.

I tucked Maddie's postcard in my mother's envelope and put all the correspondence in the back of my knapsack. When I looked for it again weeks later, I couldn't find it; it must have slipped out through a tear that had developed in the bag's lining.

AN HOUR AFTER THE announcement, I queued in the corridor and waited for the slowly moving train to arrive at the station. Ames was back in first-class, waiting to exit from that car.

I could see the lightening sky through the windows. On the pale grey platform, about thirty metres away, two men with red crosses on their arms brought a stretcher down from the train. The person on the stretcher was almost completely covered by a sheet, except for a head of auburn hair.

At the door of our car stood a uniformed railway employee. He studied the scene on the platform. "Sometimes it's hard to tell how hurt a person is," he said. "You seem fine and, then, you know."

A man approached the group on the platform. He brought his hand up to his mouth upon seeing the stretcher, and hurried toward it. When he arrived, he bent down and said something to the prone figure. She turned her head in my direction, and I recognized her as the woman we had helped. Her eyes closed, she moved slightly so that her cheek touched the man's. From their intimacy, I presumed the man was the woman's husband. An ambulance man said something to him, and he unbent himself and nodded. The two ambulance men started to walk away, carrying the stretcher. As they moved, the husband kept a hand on his wife's body as if it belonged there, like a mast on a sailboat.

AFTER THE TRAIN DEPARTED, I found Ames waiting for me at the platform's snack bar. He sat at a bistro table, smoking. I sat down and said nothing about the woman on the stretcher. We had so little time left. He would have wanted to talk about her, how we should have helped her, how we should not have left her alone, etcetera, when what I wanted to talk about was how the man on the platform kept his hand on her. I suspected Ames would say something dismissive, make me feel immature about the situation. He wouldn't understand what I wanted to say; I myself wasn't sure I could articulate what I felt. All I knew was that when I thought of that hand, I felt a return of the longing I'd been experiencing the last few weeks.

"I'll tell you why I'm going home," said Ames. "Our maid drowned. She was cleaning the pool, and she fell in." His eyes were bright.

I stopped breathing for a moment, and when I started again I was doubly aware of the smell of his cigarette smoke. "That's terrible."

"Yes." For the first time, his tone had lost all irony. He brought his cigarette toward a plastic ashtray. "My father's mistress. Trust him to hire someone who can't swim."

"That's really awful." I pictured a woman face down in a pool, her arms outstretched as if she were flying. I reached for Ames's hand, the one methodically tapping his cigarette. He let my hand linger on his wrist for a second or two before pulling it away.

I sat there. "I thought you weren't going to rescue your dad anymore."

He shrugged. "Otherwise it's *la maman* who has to deal. I'm doing it for her."

Ames smoked until he was done and then looked down the track. The next train was due at any minute.

"Hey, how long do you think it'll take for you to sort things out?" I asked him.

"I need to talk to the coroner. Contact the maid's family."

"I was thinking. Do you want to come with me?"

"You decided you need some companionship on your solo tour?" He smiled.

"After Antibes, I was thinking Spain. Or maybe Portugal. Isn't your mother from there?"

He smoked some more, then shook his head. "I can't. I have my army service to do."

My eyes prickled.

He touched my arm. "You'll be fine."

IN ANTIBES, THE SKY was blue and the houses were pink and yellow. The afternoons were long and sunny. On every surface was white light upon on which you could make shadows, experiment with versions of yourself. I walked the streets, empty because of the heat, and went to the beach. The aging ladies who sunned themselves didn't talk to me, only threw me covert glances as if to accentuate the fact that I was a stranger.

I sat in a hollowed-out place in the sand and thought about my family. I decided to call home.

My mother answered, sounding genuinely glad. She had no idea where Antibes was, she said, but she envied me the beach.

"How's Dad?"

"Fine. The doctor's cleared him for another year, at least."

I had promised myself I wouldn't ask about my sister, and yet. "How is Maddie?"

"Doing pretty well, considering." My mother sounded guarded, ready for a fight.

I felt a sudden urge for reconciliation. "You know what?

How about a visit? This hostel isn't great, but I could look for a real hotel."

"That sounds so nice. It's been years since we've taken a beach vacation."

"So come!" But what, outside my sister, could we talk about?

"It's complicated."

I didn't say anything. She would have to bring it up.

"Maddie needs to be here. With some structure."

"I meant just you and Dad."

"I know."

"Can you put Dad on the phone?" I could hear whining in my voice.

"Please don't ask him to come, Jeanne."

After we hung up, I thought of Ames, wondered what he had been asked to do to deal with the drowning. Surely he hadn't had to pull the body from the water himself. Surely, he had simply made some administrative calls and then comforted his mother.

Before parting from him, I had asked him for his number, and he had given it to me. When I dialed it, the phone rang over and over, and nobody answered.

THREE WEEKS LATER, I went home. I had slept with two more men and then stopped. Sex had started to make me feel disgusted with myself. Neither was it helping my loneliness.

When I first got home, Maddie tried to talk to me on several occasions, but stopped each time when I didn't respond. I was so damned tired of her. After six months, it was her turn to leave home. For a few weeks we heard nothing from her. Then she came back. I think it was because she had some crisis with a boyfriend. Maybe she ran out of money.

I stayed home for one year, then I left for university.

Over the next decade Maddie had her comings and goings, and a stint or two in a rehab centre. There was some talk about cocaine. I stopped paying attention. Whenever my mother called me to give the latest news, I tuned her out, cradling the phone with my shoulder as I made notes for whatever project I was working on.

One evening, while I was sitting at home reading a script, I had a sudden premonition. First I called my father's phone, but it went to voicemail. Then I tried my mother.

"Oh, Jeanne," said my mother. "What we've been going through."

Maddie had been in a coma since the morning. The emergency room doctor had told my mother that she had overdosed, probably as a result of combining alcohol and cocaine.

"You didn't think to call me?" I stared at the posters of my plays hanging from the wall of my living-room-turned-office.

"It's been a crazy day."

"I can't believe you didn't call me right away."

"Well, Jeanne, you have your own life." There was hurt in her voice, and anger. Not calling me was her revenge.

IT CROSSES MY MIND that, if I had simply been there for them, without judgment, maybe things would have been better for us.

Then I think of Ames, and the longing and the loneliness I felt again and again during those weeks of travel returns.

In the baggage car, Ames had told me that his mother had eventually decided to let his drug habit go. She even permitted him to smoke in front of her. "These days," he said, "when she has her *digestif*, I have mine. We do it together."

I picture mother and son on the stone patio of a Spanish-style house. Above them is a sky with a cutout of still white stars. Ames and his mother sit in teak armchairs, on cushions of blue and yellow cornflowers. Her legs are crossed at the ankle. They enjoy their chosen substances. They don't have to speak: it's enough that they are there, together. They are the people left behind, dealing with things as best they can.

ACKNOWLEDGEMENTS

Thank you to my first family, without whom this book would not have been born: Alain Baudot, Carla Baudot, Erica Baudot, Lucienne Baudot, René Albert Baudot, and Morris Gringorten.

Thank you to Edie Joy Sasson Gelman, chosen sister.

I am grateful to Libby Scheier, Susan Swan, and Richard Teleky, who fostered my writing years ago.

Thank you to those who, throughout the years, offered considerable editorial advice and encouragement: Sarah Selecky, Ania Szado, Sheila Toller, Jessica Westhead, and Priscila Uppal. Thank you also to Isabel Huggan and Margaret Webb for their support.

Thanks to Pietro Cammalleri for copy-editing an early version of the manuscript.

I am privileged to be a member of Meta4, my supportive and exacting band of writers: Phil Dwyer, Natalie Onuška, Phoebe Tsang.

I am grateful to have worked on this project with Bryan Ibeas, brilliant editor and generous collaborator.

Thank you to Marc Côté who took a chance with my manuscript and then fine-tuned it with a practiced eye.

Thanks to Ezra's Pound and The Green Beanery, where I wrote these stories.

I continue to find The Toronto Women's Salon invaluable for their inspiring gatherings and ongoing career advice.

Thank you to the Toronto Arts Council whose support made this book possible.

Thanks to Monica Pacheco and Rachel Letofsky at CookeMcDermid Literary Management.

Versions of these stories appeared in the literary journals *The Danforth Review*, *The Fertile Source Literary E-Zine*, and *Found Press Literary Quarterly*. Thanks to the editors of these publications.

In memory of Luke Martin and Priscila Uppal.

Laure Baudot and Cormorant Books acknowledge the sacred land on which they live and work. It has been a site of human activity for 15,000 years. This land is the territory of the Huron-Wendat and Petun First Nations, the Seneca, and most recently, the Mississaugas of the Credit River. The territory was the subject of the Dish With One Spoon Wampum Belt Covenant, an agreement between the Iroquois Confederacy and Confederacy of the Anishinaabe and allied nations to peaceably share and steward the resources around the Great Lakes. Today, the meeting place of Toronto is still home to many Indigenous people from across Turtle Island. We are grateful to have the opportunity to work in the community, on this territory.

We are also mindful of broken covenants and the need to strive to make right with all our relations.